To Bob, my favorite running back.

JAR Jarecki, Amy, author.
Defenseless **FRA**

9/2021

Defenseless

A Stand-Alone College Sports Romance

by

Amy Jarecki

ST. MARY PARISH LIBRARY
FRANKLIN, LOUISIANA

All rights reserved.

No part of this publication may be sold, copied, distributed, reproduced, or transmitted in any form by any means, mechanical or digital, including photocopying and recording or by any information storage and retrieval system without the prior written permission of the author Amy Jarecki, except in the case of brief quotations embodied in critical articles and reviews.

PUBISHER'S NOTE: This is a work of fiction. Names, characters, places, and incidents either are the product of the author's imagination or are used factiously. Any resemblance to actual persons living or dead, business establishments, events or locales is entirely coincidental.

Copyright © 2021 Amy Jarecki

ISBN: 9781942442394

Chapter One

Cade

The toxic silence in the courtroom speared through my lungs, pinning me to the chair. Nervous sweat chafed my pits. An eternity passed with every tick from the clock on the wall, ratcheting up my anxiety while my attorney fidgeted beside me. Barely able to breathe, I stared at the door to the right of the bench, wanting this to be over yet terrified of the outcome.

My gut was wound so tight, I'd spent the past hour frozen in place, willing myself not to puke. I rubbed my sweaty palms on my suit pants. Even though a year had slipped away since my arrest, I still couldn't believe I'd been accused of a crime I did not commit.

Since that day I've wallowed in the fires of hell.

And hell shows no mercy.

Expelled from school, all my dreams went down the crapper with an allegation from a woman I once considered a friend.

That's right. For just over twelve months I've faced the wicked irony of being guilty until proven innocent.

A loud click echoed through the overcrowded courtroom, making me jolt. Bile burned my throat. Gulping, I watched as the jury filed inside and took their seats. A few glanced my way. An elderly lady even smiled, though sadness was reflected in her eyes.

God save me, this was my moment of truth—*or not*. In the next minute, my life might be over.

All hope lost.

My heart raced, my breathing sped and, if I'd eaten breakfast, I'd be hurling eggs and bacon across the table. Might even soil my attorney's Armani shoes. Here I sat, twenty-one years of age, staring ten years or more of hard time dead in the face. My self-esteem, my plans, my future blasted into oblivion.

And don't tell me any different.

Yeah, my attorney presented the evidence with unabashed confidence. He was good. The best. My case was strong, but the courtroom was filled with people who wanted to sever my balls and crush them in a vise. They didn't care if the sex was consensual or not. They didn't care about the kissy texts or the misunderstanding that followed.

They didn't care about *my* side.

They were like a pack of wolves tracking my scent. To them I was guilty as sin, not because I might have committed a crime, but because they wanted to bag a college starting tight end who, before a year ago, had a sure-fire shot at being a first-round draft pick in the NFL.

"Has the jury reached a verdict?" asked the judge, his voice ominous.

The foreperson stood. "We have, your honor."

"Will the defendant please rise."

The last thing I wanted to do was stand in front of this mob of vultures. If only I could turn around and tell them exactly what I thought of their messed-up idea of due process. But the man beside me tapped my elbow and gave me a nod. Somehow I got to my feet, locking my knees to ensure I didn't fall on my face.

I tugged at my collar. My tie choked me, my sports coat felt like a straitjacket infused with smoldering coals. And with the blast of heat, a bead of sweat rolled down my temple.

The bailiff handed the judge an envelope. Taking it, the old man squinted at me over the rims of his glasses as he pulled out a slip of paper and read. After clearing his throat, he shifted his attention to the foreperson. "What say you?"

Shaking, I stared straight ahead, unable to exhale, unable to fucking think.

"We find the defendant, Cade Riley Williams, not guilty."

The courtroom erupted in an ear-splitting banter of cheers and boos. But for me, everything spun. I planted my palms on the table as my knees buckled and sweat drained into my eyes. This was the best news I'd heard in eons but I was still trembling, feeling as if I were being sucked deeper into the vortex of hell.

My attorney clapped me on the back, grinning like he'd won the lottery. "I told you we had an ironclad case, son."

Yeah, he'd been confident all along, but it hadn't been his ass on the line. I hated to admit it, but this was a high-profile case and winning would make him big bucks not only from me, but from all the defendants out there who needed a miracle. The deal? He'd represent me, get me back into school and on the team. Then, once I graduated, I'd start paying his six-figure fee whether or not I went pro.

Shitty bargain being forced to defend myself for loving someone.

But right now, in my book the man was nothing short of a saint.

"You okay?" he asked.

I cracked a smile. "I'm dazed."

"To be expected." He shook my hand. "Congratulations."

"Can we slip out the side door and avoid the drama?" I knew it wasn't going to be pretty. Sure, a lot of my teammates and supporters were here, but I swear they were outnumbered ten-to-one. Every time I'd been to court I had to face the reporters—and the protesters. Hell, I have two sisters. I'm one of the first people in line to support women's rights, but try to tell that to the hyena who was sitting behind me during the trial, mumbling hate accusations under her breath—loud enough for me to hear but too soft to be caught by the judge.

And no one needed to tell me this wasn't over. I still had the dean of Madison University to contend with. I still had to convince Coach I was fit to rejoin the team. And I needed to walk out of here without being shot.

Back home in Jersey they'd shot my dad for far less.

Why not me?

So many things could still go wrong. Yet I had to stand tall and face them like a man. I owed it to my father and, if he were watching in heaven, I'd damned-well make him proud.

"You ready?" asked my attorney.

I put on my game face and tugged down my sports coat. "Hell, yeah."

But walking outside was worse than running onto the field at Ohio while 105,000 fans booed at the top of their lungs. Right now, the spectators weren't exactly booing but plenty of them were staring at me like I was a rattlesnake coiled and ready to strike.

My attorney grabbed my elbow and turned his lips to my ear. "Remember, put on the show of your life. Don't blame anyone. Tell them how thankful you are to receive justice. And make sure you say how much you're looking forward to returning to Madison whether or not you're allowed back on the team."

"Got it," I said through gritted teeth. I knew the drill.

I'd been biting my tongue for months. Regardless of how much I wanted to point my finger and reinforce my innocence, I had to play it cool. I had to give press the best acting job of my life. Tell them I was only looking to the future from here on out. Let bygones be bygones. Who cared if throughout the trial the media took the plaintiff's side and ignored mine?

Yeah, right.

One day I'd let them know how I really felt.

Just not today.

Probably not until after I graduated.

If the dean rescinds my expulsion and allows me to return. Otherwise, I'm screwed.

Outside on the courthouse steps the questions all came at once. My attorney fielded most of them but he deferred to me about the future.

My lines rehearsed, I stood my ground. "I just want to get back to school and hit the books. Play ball if I can."

Then someone asked how much it hurt to know I'd lost millions of dollars when my pro career went down the drain.

Bastard.

Eyeing the ruthless idiot, I clenched my fists, my entire body ready to lunge forward and plant a jab in the shithead's snout.

"Enough questions for now," said my attorney, wrapping his arm around my shoulders as if he knew I was about to explode. "A formal statement will be issued. I will be contacting Madison University forthwith to demand Mr. William's reinstatement."

He led me toward the curb and into a limo. Once we reached his office I thanked him and his assistant, donned my helmet, and hopped on my Harley.

"What are you going to do to celebrate?" he asked.

Stay away from women.

"Go for a *long* ride," I said as I turned the key and revved the motor.

Through town I idled at the speed limit but when I hit County Road K, I stepped on the gas. With no one in sight, I clocked up a century on the straight, only slowing to take the turn onto Highway Twelve. A couple more turns and I hit the dirt road skirting Devil's Lake. Late summer, it hadn't rained in a while and my rear tire fishtailed in the dust. As I countered with the handlebars, it took all my strength to keep the bike upright.

But it felt damned good.

I fought the Harley like it was a demon, turning left, right, and skidding around a hairpin turn. Without putting my foot down, I continued up, the tires spinning, rocks kicking out beneath them.

I should be shouting for joy, but I couldn't get past the rage pulsing through my blood. I'd lost a year of my life. I still might have lost my chances to play ball. To be a pro.

I missed my dad.

Mom, too.

I should have let her fly in from Jersey. But I couldn't have faced her if the verdict didn't go my way. She was a good woman and raised me right. She didn't deserve to lose her husband *and* her son.

Right before I reached the cliff I spun the bike, swerving to a stop. I cut the motor and ripped off my helmet.

Down below, the lake looked like glass without a boat in sight, thank God.

"Gaaaaaaaaaaaa!" I bellowed until my throat burned.

But the pain didn't stop me. I picked up a good-sized rock and hurled it from the cliff. "Fuck you baaaaaaaaastards!"

"I am innocent! I. Am. Goddamned. Innocent!"

My chest constricted like I'd been hit by a two hundred eighty-pound linebacker. What hurt the most? So many people I'd never met condemned me before they knew the facts—before they knew *me*.

I prided myself on being a good man. But my integrity had gotten me nowhere.

Tears stung my eyes as I dropped to my knees, my fists yanking my hair. "I am innocent!" I croaked like an adolescent.

Tears streamed from my eyes while damned sobs wracked my body as if the agony I'd carried inside for so long was ripping me apart.

I was so fucking messed up.

My attorney would probably be successful in getting me back into Madison University. If so, how would I face my teammates? How could I show myself in class?

Most of all, how in God's name was I going to reassemble the shreds of my pride and restart my miserable life?

Chapter Two

Vivian

Three weeks later.

I slung my yoga mat over my shoulder and opened my mailbox—number 914, second from the last. Peering inside, my heart gave a little zing when I found an envelope from the tutoring office addressed to Vivian Ellis.

"Thank God," I mumbled under my breath, running my finger under the top edge and pulling out the letter. I needed this job—anything to help with my mounting tuition costs. It was my senior year and my debt already looked as bad as a mortgage.

Sure, I had an academic scholarship and some financial aid. But those didn't cover my expenses by half.

Heading toward the elevators, I shook out the paper. Then a lead ball sank to the pit of my stomach.

I froze dead in my tracks while my mouth went dry. "No. Way."

"Hey!" said a guy stumbling around me. "Don't stop like that unless you want to be bowled over."

I gave him a sideways glance. "Sorry."

Still grimacing, I held the letter against my chest so no one could see it and ducked into the elevator.

"Bad news?" asked the guy. I'd seen him before. Sophomore, I think.

My shoulder ticked up. "Good and bad."

He got off on the fifth floor, then I continued to the ninth—to the same dorm room I'd shared with Lisa since freshman year.

Inside, she was bent over toweling her hair dry. She gave me an upside-down grin. "Vi!"

"Hey." I shut the door, collapsed on my bed, and groaned. "I got my tutoring assignment."

"Cool," she said, tossing the towel on the carpet and reaching for her brush. "I *think*. You don't sound too excited about it."

"That's because I'm freaking out."

Needing something to do, I hopped up, grabbed the towel, dipped into the bathroom, and neatly draped it over the rod. No matter how many times I'd asked Lisa to hang up her disgusting things, she deluded herself into believing the floor was a suitable towel rack. I stopped saying anything midway through our junior year after ignoring a pile of towels for an entire week...until I couldn't stand the mess for another second.

Yeah, I'm a little OCD, but I like her no matter what. Lisa is the best roomie ever. She even hangs up her clothes.

Most of the time.

The messy nut calls me a neat freak, but the situation somehow works for us.

She met me on my way out of the bathroom, her big blue eyes unblinking and looking about as shocked as I felt. "Freaked out?"

"Yeah." I gulped, my gaze shifting to the letter on the bed. "Think of the most notorious football player in the country." Heck, I might not even have realized Madison had a football team if it weren't for Cade William's face on the news and in the papers every other day.

Lisa's jaw dropped. "No way."

I pushed past her, grabbed the note, and shoved it under her nose. "Read for yourself."

When she glanced down, her eyes bulged. "Oh my God."

With the paper still in my hand, I sat on my bed, grabbed my Aquaman pillow, and hugged it across my midriff. "Right?"

"Are you going to do it?"

My gaze slid to the weekly wages listed at the bottom of the letter. Lord knew I needed the money—and the pay was higher than I'd expected. "I thought I'd be assigned to a freshman."

"Well, if you don't feel safe, you ought to refuse."

Easy for Lisa to say. Her dad was the head of a major law firm in Chicago. He paid out-of-state tuition and it barely dented his bank account. I rubbed my nose over my pillow's lavender-scented blue velvet. "Cade *was* acquitted," I reasoned.

"True, but we all know he's no saint. He had a reputation on campus even before he was expelled."

"Expelled and then reinstated after the dean reviewed the court docs." I dropped onto my back and stared at the ceiling. "You, yourself, said the university's guidelines were stricter than a court of law's."

"I did." Lisa worked a comb through the ends of her long blonde hair—she had it all—brains, a cute bod, and gorgeous hair. "But just today I read an article about how college athletes slip through the cracks by transferring out of state." Though she was brilliant and pre-law, her argument didn't always make sense.

I rolled to my side, propping my head in my palm. "But Williams is still attending Madison. He didn't transfer to a different school or state."

She shook her head. "It still could be dangerous. You know I care about you."

"I know you care. But if the dude were truly dangerous, I don't think the board would have let him come back. After all, he had already been expelled. It would have been easy for them to deny his reinstatement."

"So, you're gonna do it?"

Visions of my measly bank account balance pirouetted through my head. "I don't have much of a choice."

"This is insane." Lisa paced, then whipped around and speared her pointer finger through the air, straight at my face. "Promise me you'll call 911 if you even have a whisper of doubt."

I threw the pillow at her. "A whisper?"

She caught it and swung Aquaman's face above her head, making like she was about to pummel me with it. "Promise!"

"But—"

Thwack! She planted Jason Momoa between my eyes, slamming my glasses up the bridge of my nose. "Promise, or I'll go with you."

God, that would be almost as embarrassing as having my mom there looking over my shoulder. I mean, I was a tutor. The person in charge. I don't need an escort.

Lisa pulled back the pillow, readying for another blow.

I threw my hands in front of my face. "Okay, okay! I'll keep my phone in my pocket."

"Keep it beside you on the desk. Then all you have do to is hit the panic button."

"Fine."

She tossed Aquaman to the foot of my bed. "I can't believe they lumbered you with *him*."

I rolled over and stretched my back in the sleeping swan yoga position. "I can't believe a dude like Williams is taking accounting."

"Makes sense to me. All pro athletes need some sort of business sense." Lisa started toward the bathroom. "Let's eat after I finish getting ready."

When the hair dryer turned on, I eased back to my butt and released a long exhale. Seriously, this assignment ought to be a walk in the park—good money and all I needed to do was tutor for an hour four days per week. Except I'd be showing Cade Williams how to draw a T-chart with debits and credits.

Cade Williams.

He not only had a reputation as a bad boy footballer, girls were known to swoon whenever he walked past. I didn't follow sports, but I'd heard about fanatical women who hung out in the tunnel after practice just to get a look at him—and the others, of course. But Williams was probably one of the few who looked like he belonged on a Hollywood movie set with America's most gorgeous.

I folded up the letter and slipped it into my backpack.

Thank God I wasn't the type to go weak-kneed over a guy. I was a serious student and good enough to be accepted into the tutoring program.

I pulled out my lip gloss, moved to the mirror and applied it, then smacked my lips, wondering if I ought to wear contacts for the tutoring sessions. Nah. I only had a few free packets my optometrist gave me when I ordered my glasses, and I saved those for nice. Problem was, nice rarely ever came.

The truth? The head of the accounting department probably recommended me for this assignment because he knew I wouldn't go gaga and neither would Williams. I wasn't and would never be his type.

That's right.

Every session, I'd go in with a lesson plan, check his work, and mind my own freaking business.

Easy.

Chapter Three

Cade

I stood with my face upturned to the spray of hot water. God, the receiver's coach worked our asses off today. But I needed it. I needed anything to take my mind off...*everything*.

I turned and let the water pulse across my shoulders.

Being back at Madison felt awkward as hell. Even at today's practice it seemed as if I were on the outside looking in through a barrier of bulletproof glass. My bro, Jason, and the O-line stood beside me, but I caught the accusing glances from some freshmen and a few defensive players. I knew half of them were wondering why I'd been reinstated. The other half? They were probably wondering if I'd rip their heads off if they flapped their mouths.

They had no idea that I would have endured any abuse to stay on the team.

Any.

I'd kept in shape during the year I'd spent in purgatory. Sure, I could handle all the cardio and weights my trainer in Jersey could throw at me, but I couldn't replicate running plays. Without a team I'd gone "football soft". No matter how much I worked out, ran routes, and caught passes from my trainer, it wasn't the same as being out there on the field taking hits.

Especially now that everything had changed.

On the field I had something to prove now more than ever. Not only to the coaches and my teammates, but to myself. I was going to be the best damned tight end Madison had ever seen, or kill myself trying.

Despite all the drama, I had two goals this year.

Two goals I was determined to achieve.

The first was easy—give the team everything I've got and help win a major bowl game. The second was to show the dean I wasn't some flunky football player. She'd arched her eyebrows when she mentioned my past grades were barely acceptable for reinstatement. I might have been flying by the seat of my pants before. But never again.

I wasn't a dumbass and, after spending the last year pumping gas and living with my mom, the value of education jettisoned to number two on my list. Screw the parties. When the board had initially rescinded my expulsion, I still didn't know if I'd be back on the team. Getting approval from the NCAA took another week of nail-biting but when the news finally came I swore on my father's grave I would not be working at a gas station for the rest of my life.

I'm going to make something of myself be it on the field or in business.

Hopefully, both.

I turned off the water, grabbed a towel, and tucked it around my waist.

"Hey bro," said Jason Allen—ace wide receiver and the best friend a guy like me ever had. He was the only one who'd regularly stayed in touch while I was fighting for my innocence. "Good practice. You looked like a man out there."

"Thanks." I gave him a fist bump. "Those reps nearly killed me."

"Coach nearly killed everyone. Says to beat Ohio we have to be able to run sprints for two hours nonstop."

Heading for my locker, I threw a sly smirk over my shoulder. "Didn't we do that today?"

"Sure feels like it." Jason followed, making a grunting noise in the back of his throat. I knew that noise. Maybe I'd missed it too. The sound meant he had more to say and was thinking about how to phrase it.

I quickly cranked the dial on my lock and popped it. "So, what's up?"

He leaned against the neighboring locker and crossed his ankles. "You know all the brothers are happy to have you back."

A pent-up breath whistled through my lips. "I sure hope so."

"They are. We all feel for you, bro. What happened to you was a nightmare."

Damn, even Jason didn't know the half of it. Here I was six-five, weighing in at two-fifty and I walked around campus constantly looking over my shoulder. Worse, I'd do anything for a decent night's sleep. "Tell me about it."

"Well, the offense got together to decide how to celebrate your reinstatement. Decision is we're throwing you a party. Devan's hosting. At eight tomorrow. Wednesday in case you didn't know."

Groaning, I rubbed my neck. "Seriously, dude?" Sure, I used to be the renowned life at any jam. But now, I just wanted to lay low. "Maybe we should hold off on the parties for a while."

"I know coming back has to be harder than climbing Everest. But the guys want to do something to show you how psyched they are that you beat the odds. I promise we won't keep you up late, princess." Jason punched my shoulder. "Besides, you need to get back in the saddle, and the sooner you start the better you'll feel."

"That so?"

"Yeah." He pounded his fist on the locker. "Tomorrow night at eight. You'd better show up."

I watched him head down the corridor before I slid into my jeans and a faded Madison t-shirt. The weather was too warm for a hoodie but I still put one on and tugged the hood low over my brow. No use advertising my identity while I sprinted across campus.

I'd worry about the party later. Right now, I had five minutes to get to my tutoring session. I've never had a tutor in my life, but the dean said if I wanted to bring up my GPA, one-on-one sessions would help.

At this stage what the dean wanted the dean got. And why not? Spending my weeknights studying ought to keep me out of trouble.

Arriving in the library foyer one minute late, I stopped in my tracks when a brown-haired girl stepped in front of me. "Cade Williams?" she asked, her voice soft and kind of sultry. Possibly unsure as well.

My jaw twitched as I gave a single nod.

"I'm Vivian Ellis." She was tall for a girl, probably five-ten. Smooth skin. Glasses. Curves... I wiped my eyes as she motioned me to follow. "I've reserved a study room if that's okay."

This was my tutor? Seriously? Despite her height, she looked young enough to be fresh out of high school. "Um...yeah, sure."

"Good."

She led the way with a stack of books wrapped in her arms and a backpack slung over her shoulder.

I threw out my hand. "Let me carry those."

"I'm fine."

I stepped in front of her, making her stop. She looked up, her brown eyes round and cautious beneath those black-rimmed fames. Then she quickly glanced away. Great. Either I intimidated her or she really was right out of high school.

"Are you some kind of genius?" I asked.

Vivian rolled her eyes to the ceiling as if she got asked that question every-other day. "Never took an IQ test."

I slid the books from her arms. "I only asked because you look like a freshman." Possibly younger. "I expected someone *older*." Maybe male. Maybe a dude who acted like Mr. Rogers.

Leading on, she huffed and shook her head. "I suggest we refrain from talking about anything except accounting."

I followed, trying not to notice the view from behind. Dammit, I could care less about her ass. "Fine by me." Heart-shaped, not too big, not too small...

Stop you idiot!

She'd actually given me sass. Maybe I'd finally met someone who didn't want to ask me a gazillion questions about the trial.

Miss Sass-Bomb pushed into a small room with a table and four chairs and ushered me in. "Put the books on the table." She faced me with her hands on her hips—clad in snug-fitting jeans, topped by an over-sized pink tee with a scooped neck which had managed to slip its way off her shoulder. "I'm an accounting major, a *senior*, and I don't give a fig about football. Got it?"

I arched my eyebrow at the bare shoulder—skin like polished silk. "Sure," I said as she yanked her shirt up with a glare that immediately rearranged my priorities.

Thank God, Vivian Ellis was exactly the type of tutor I needed. She just might be the queen of the soreheads. Hell, I bet she'd never flirted a day in her life. I also figured I didn't need to recite my bio. Even if she didn't watch football, after all my publicity, a student would have to have been locked in a closet not to know.

"Good, then let's get started." She sat and gestured to a chair beside her. "How much accounting have you had?"

I was ready to dig in, except when I took the seat, she smelled like the ocean—like flowers and honeysuckle and anything other than a teacher. My first-grade teacher, Mrs. Fink, was older than dirt and smelled like granny perfume. Why not Miss Sass-Bomb?

Gritting my teeth, I tugged off my hoodie, taking a good whiff of the fabric softener I'd used yesterday. No way I'd let some insipid perfume throw me off my game.

"This is my virgin voyage," I said, answering her question. "And I need an A."

Then I planted my forehead in my palm. Why did I have to say virgin?

"All right." Opening one of her enormous books, I swear she checked out my pecs from the corner of her eye as she pointed to columns of numbers. "We'll begin with debits and credits."

In a blink, she focused on nothing but the book as she gave me a concise intro.

By the time she was done, all tension had dispersed from the room. It was like she'd entered her zone and was totally focused on the lesson.

Watching her made it easy to concentrate. Listen, too. Vivian's voice commanded my attention. Not in an irritating way, but her tone enticed me. She explained things so clearly, making it impossible not to understand. And she was all business. I pictured her wearing a navy suit with those chestnut locks up in a tight bun. If she shifted her glasses low on her nose and pursed those full lips, she'd probably be a knockout in any boardroom. Nope. There'd be no sassing Vivian Ellis else she'd tackle you with a brown-eyed stare. Probably give you an eyeball concussion while she was at it.

After the lesson, she tucked her hair behind her ear, reverting to the girl I saw when I'd first arrived at the library. She even smiled. "Good work today. We got further than I'd planned."

Yeah, she'd probably assumed I wasn't too bright. Hopefully, she'd change her opinion by the end of the semester. In fact, I wanted her to. "Thanks," I replied before I was hit by the stupidest idea I'd ever had. But I didn't bother to check myself. My right brain took over and insisted it was brilliant. "So, Vivian..."

"Call me Vi. Everyone else does."

"Okay." My gut clenched like I was about to run sixty yards up the field for a Hail Mary pass. "Um, the team—well, not the entire team, but the offensive players—"

Shaking her head, she gave me a blank stare. "The what?"

I blinked twice. Wow, she really didn't know jack shit about the game. I ignored her question and continued, "Ah...some of the guys are throwing a party for me tomorrow night."

"Why am I not surprised?" she asked, folding her arms and frowning. Maybe she didn't know anything about football, but she certainly was clued in on my reputation—that is, my *prior* reputation.

I hesitated for a moment while she stared at me, her eyes too gorgeous, and way too accusing. Or were they too hypnotic? In any case, I needed to stop staring into those damned eyes.

Besides, this plan was about the best thing I could come up with in the next twenty-four hours. My gaze shifted to her lips as I rubbed the back of my neck. Hell, the lips weren't any better. Before I got myself in trouble, I focused on the accounting book and drilled my two goals into my brain—*football and grades*. Period.

"Anyway," I continued. "There are always girls at these things."

"Girls? Go figure." She snorted. "I'm guessing that's a problem."

"Yeah, and I was wondering if…well…" I glanced at her glasses—big, dark, cute. "If you'd be willing to go with me?"

Her eyes lit up for a moment, then she smirked. "Right. To protect you from the nasty mean girls?"

"They're not mean." I couldn't believe I'd just said that after one of the very same had practically ruined my life. "Well, I'll admit some are. But, in my book, they're *all* off limits."

"Hmm." Vi looked down at her chest. I tried not to follow her gaze, but I couldn't help checking out those curves. Oh, yeah. She was well-formed under that loose-fitting T. Hell, no guy on the planet could ignore those tits—not even when said guy was focusing on accounting. "In case you haven't noticed, I *am* a girl."

Yeah, maybe I did notice a little too much, but something about Vivian Ellis told me to keep my hands to myself—as if she were above me. I could use someone like her at my six even if she made me nervous—not that I'd admit that a made me nervous. "I mean…um…" How could I explain my game plan? "I'd think *you* wouldn't be there to flirt. You said yourself you don't care about football."

Dropping her head back, her shoulders shook with a sarcastic laugh. "So, you want me to be your bodyguard?"

I cracked up, imagining my tutor blocking a two-hundred-pound corner so I could make a play.

She stacked up her books and stood. "So, is this all some sort of joke?"

"No...ah...but the idea of you being my bodyguard is ludicrous. *However,* if I'm with you, those so-called 'mean girls' will stay away." I bit my lip giving her my best pleading puppy dog eyes.

She didn't cave. "Let me get this straight. If you have your tutor on your arm you'll be able to resist temptation?"

Exactly. "That's the idea." Maybe I still had a chance. "Look, I totally don't want to go to the party, but I'll let my brothers down if I don't show. I know it sounds psycho because we just met, but I'm comfortable with you. I feel like I can trust you."

"Wow." She pulled out her cell phone and lit up the screen. "Comfort and trust in an hour. I must be better at this tutoring thing than I thought."

Yeah, Vi could dish out sass, but she hadn't said no and it was time to seal the deal. "Pick you up at seven-thirty, okay?"

Vi shoved the phone back in her rear jeans pocket. "Why not?"

Thank. God.

After I got her number and address, I again pulled on my hoodie and we headed out while I carried the books.

Well before we reached the door, I spotted a mob of people crowding the foyer and ducked behind a row of bookshelves. "Oh no."

"What?"

I inclined my head toward the pack. "Someone must have seen me come in here."

Vi tsked her tongue. "Cripes, I knew something like this would happen."

Cripes? I would have burst out laughing if we weren't about to be mobbed. I checked for exit signs but there wasn't much to see besides an alley of books. "Is there another way out of here?"

Grabbing my hand, she pulled me toward the wall. "Back door. Down a flight."

I tightened my grip as I spotted the stairs and took the lead. I could have let go, but I wanted to keep her close. Vi didn't have to get mixed up in this mess and help me. She could have pointed me in the right direction and left me to my own devices, but something told me she wasn't that kind of girl. No, someone who cared enough to be a tutor had integrity—a sense of duty.

Maybe she even liked me a little. I mean *me*. Not the notorious celebrity I'd become.

More probable, she withheld judgement. I guess I'd do the same.

"It's dark," I said as we stepped outside. "Let me walk you home."

She reached for her books but I shifted them away from her grasp. "No need. I'm staying in Prentiss Hall."

"A dorm?" I hadn't paid any attention to her address when she wrote it down but I didn't know one single upperclassman who still lived in a dorm. "I thought you said you were a senior."

Vi shrugged as she moved along. Fast. "I like being on campus. I can sleep longer."

"But you have to deal with adolescent underclassmen."

"I suppose. I've had the same roommate since freshman year so that makes it bearable."

I stopped in the shadows outside Prentiss and returned her books. "So, I'll see you tomorrow?"

"It's a date." Cringing, she shook her head and swept away her comment by waving her palm like a windshield wiper on hyperdrive. "Sorry. Wrong word. It's a-an *appointment*. How's that?"

One corner of my mouth turned up. I moved to brush my knuckle across her cheek but stopped myself in time and shoved my fist into my jeans' pocket. "Sure. I promise not to be late for our *appointment*, Miss Ellis."

Chapter Four

Vivian

Oh. My. God.

My mind raced as I grabbed a tray in the dining hall. I was practically hyperventilating, my body zinging everywhere.

I could have been floating for all I knew.

And I shouldn't be. I darn well should not have said yes.

But I did.

I had just agreed to go to a party with a bunch of oversexed, musclebound football players, and act as Cade's bodyguard.

Chick repellant was more apt.

I smirked at the idiocy. As if he thought having me there would work for more than two seconds. I might be tall, but I was a non-violent yoga nut. No matter what he may have thought, I hadn't attended Madison with blinders on. I knew what cheerleaders, dance team members, and football groupie girls looked like.

Gorgeous.

They worked at being hotties day and night.

Me?

A swipe of eye pencil, a tad of mascara, some lip gloss, and I called it good. And most mornings I just gave up on my hair. No lie, I ranked with the best of the best when it came to bad hair days.

Those football player magnet chicks would laugh as they pushed me aside and glommed onto Cade. I knew he was a tight end because that's what the papers had reported. And though I didn't have a clue what a tight end was actually supposed to do, it didn't take a genius to figure out he caught the ball. Evidently, he was a very efficient ball catcher.

But I didn't think the girls cared too much about his talent.

One look at the dude and anyone would swoon.

I sure did *in spite* of warning myself not to throughout the entire day.

When he'd opened the door to the library, the air had whooshed from my lungs. And that was before he even glanced my way. I was so petrified, I'd had to force myself to gulp prior to stepping forward and introducing myself. And once we'd gone into the study room I tried my best not to look at him.

Aside from the odd stolen glimpse, I mostly kept my focus on the book. Thank goodness I know my stuff. Knowledge was the only thing that had prevented me from melting into a gooey heap. As he sat beside me, I felt like a moth drawn to a flame—the most bewitching, alluring, tempting flame I'd ever been near. Except being the dude's tutor, every single feeling buzzing through my body was utterly wrong.

Gah!

I needed to get over it—like yesterday. I'm not supposed to see him outside of our sessions. Well, there isn't exactly a rule forbidding fraternization, but tutors don't socialize with their students. It's just too weird.

As I moved around the deli kiosk, I grabbed a salad. I must have stood there dazed because the guy behind me gave me a nudge, then I blindly went on to the next station.

Why did I agree to go to the imbecilic party? I'm such a dupe! One look at Cade's pale blue eyes and I caved. Cripes, Mother Theresa would have caved.

I'd never been to a football player's party before. Honestly, I wasn't much of a party animal. Quiet get-togethers with my fellow accounting majors was more my style. Though I have to admit my crowd wasn't as tame as outsiders thought.

Still, I'll be like a carp out of water, my eyes stunned and shifting unblinkingly while I gasp for air. Worse, I had no idea what I'd wear. A business suit so I looked like a tutor?

A dress was out of the question.

Whatever I choose, I definitely must not attract attention. Fading into the shadows was more my style. And I wasn't going to hang on Cade's arm like some lovesick tutoress. If he needed me to rescue him, he could darn well come over and hang on *my* arm.

After grabbing more food and plopping it on my tray, I swiped my card and headed for the table Lisa and I shared with the few seniors still dorming it.

"Hey," I said, sliding into a seat. "Where is everyone?"

Lisa shrugged. "Pizza, maybe? No one texted me."

I shoved a bite of salad into my mouth. "Me neither."

"Are you on a new diet?"

"Huh?"

She flicked my lemon meringue pie plate. "Salad and *five* desserts? What gives?"

I stopped mid-chew and looked down. Holy crap. What was I thinking? "Um...they looked so good I thought I'd taste-test them all." Best excuse I could come up with in two seconds.

"But you've tried every dessert on the campus about a gazillion times."

"Not this year."

She dug into her lasagna. Lisa's food looked a whole lot more appetizing than my salad, especially since I'd forgotten to add dressing.

"So, how was your tutoring session?" she asked.

I jolted, making the salad bowl flip and covering the Bavarian chocolate cake with lettuce. "Fine," I said, while a blast of heat sprang up my face. Covering, I snatched a few pieces of romaine and shoved them into my mouth.

Lisa leaned in. "That bad, huh?"

"N-no," I squeaked, not sounding like me at all. "We went straight through the lesson and he followed along intently. I even think he might have learned something."

"Hmm." Lisa sipped her Mango Lacroix. "Sounds like it was pretty normal."

I sliced the cake with the side of my fork and knocked my Jell-O off the table. "Absolutely. Yes." My voice still sounded like a pre-teen while I tried to ignore the fact that I had suddenly turned into an utter klutz.

"I know you're strung like a harp string most of the time, but I've never seen you this psycho." She leaned over and gaped at the red goo wobbling on the stark-white floor tiles. "Something went down. I can tell. Now spill it."

Unable to leave the Jell-O where it landed, I swooped down with my napkin, grabbed the glob, and deposited it into my salad bowl.

Lisa wrapped her fingers around my wrist and squeezed. "Stop fidgeting for one second and tell me what happened. Do I need to call the campus police?"

"Oh, no, nothing like that. He..."

Releasing her grip, she rolled her hand through the air, demanding more.

"It's no big deal, really," I explained in a rush. "The guys—the *offense*, he said, whatever that is, is throwing him a party tomorrow night and he asked me if I'd come along and be his bodyguard."

My best friend's jaw dropped. "Bodyguard? Are you serious?"

Cade needed my help. And how could I resist that face? It was like staring a baby Chihuahua in the eyes and saying there would be no cuddles today. Maybe Chihuahua wasn't the right puppy dog. Bull Mastiff might fit. A Chocolate Retriever puppy?

Anyway, I ignored Lisa's sarcasm. "Well, chick repellant is more like it. He wants the groupie-girls to stay away from him and he can't exactly not show up for a party thrown in his honor."

"Your reasoning is totally insane," she said like a true pre-law major.

Of course, I'd thought the same. Why on earth would Cade Williams need me to tag along to some stupid party where I have no chance of fitting in? They'd probably use a bunch of football jargon and I'd be clueless. Then they'd snigger behind their backs, "*Look at Vi, the four-eyed accounting nerd.*"

Lisa planted her palms on the table and leaned in. "Did he say anything about being *your* bodyguard? Good Lord, girl, not only is *he* six-five, he is huge enough to completely crush you, no matter if you are five-ten. And talk about chick magnets, there's the quarterback, Devan Thomas—

he's up for a Heisman and he's just as hot as Cade if you ask me. Need I remind you of Jason Allen, *your* student's best friend, Bo Jakes, only the most awesome running back in the country, not to mention Gary—"

"Wait!" I jammed the heels of my hands against my temples. "You're no football nut. How do you know all this stuff?"

"I read the Gyrfalcon News. Don't you? Besides, it's all the pre-law dudes talk about, not to mention if you want to bond with my dad during football season you have to know the game."

"Seriously? Why did I not know this before today?"

"Football isn't exactly at the top of *my* priority list." Lisa crushed her Lacroix can in her fist. "But that's not what we're talking about. Cade asked you out during your first tutoring session? I knew he was a jerk."

"No." My spine jolted ramrod straight. "It wasn't like that at all. He's trying to lay low and he said there are always girls at those parties. And I understand. He doesn't want to get involved with *anyone* right now."

"Yeah right. Tell me he didn't notice your tits."

I crossed my arms over my boobs and glared. So, my boobs were a tad on the large side…kinda like my ass. "I'm his *tutor*, okay? Decorum dictates our relationship is purely platonic."

"Decorum? You're talking about bad-boy Cade Williams. Next you'll be telling me he's the most chivalric dude on campus."

He seemed chivalrous to me. After all, he didn't need to walk me back to the dorm. Or carry my books. He could have even told me where to meet him before the party tomorrow, but instead he'd said he'd pick me up. That behavior didn't seem ignoble to me.

Lisa drummed her fingers together as if she were plotting. "Well, if you're going to this thing, you absolutely cannot show up looking like a Brainiac. They'll eat you alive. We're totally going to have to do a makeover. Besides, I loaded up on the new colors over the summer."

"Jeez, don't you think that's overkill? I thought I'd try to look kinda plain-Jane-ish." I twirled an errant lock of hair around my finger. "Do you really think a makeover is necessary?"

"Absolutely. Besides, it's MAC and I will make you look like a supermodel."

Lisa had the goods to look like a supermodel but she usually didn't put a whole lot of effort into it unless she was seeing some hot graduate student.

"This isn't a date," I moaned. "I don't want to look like a supermodel."

"Shut up." She stood and pulled me to my feet, leaving all five desserts uneaten. "You also need a crash course on football terms. I swear, between tonight and tomorrow that's all we'll have time for."

Chapter Five

Cade

Wednesdays were the only weeknights I didn't have a tutoring session and I felt awkward pushing through the doors of Prentiss Hall to meet my tutor. But I'd invited Vi and I suppose I needed her, so I stuck with the plan and made a bee-line for the desk while the swarm of residents cleared a path. "Vivian Ellis, room 914, please."

"You Mr. Williams?" The dude looked up and did a double take. "Holy—"

"She's expecting me," I said, waiting for a smart reply. Everyone had one.

"She sure is." He grinned and handed me a visitor tag. "She left you a pass."

I'd sort of expected Vi to be waiting in the lobby, but then that hadn't been discussed. Honestly, I didn't mind going up to get her, but this wasn't a date. Even though I was wearing a ball cap, I felt like a target. I clipped the tag to my shirt. "Thanks."

"No prob, dude. Hey, welcome back."

I gave him a thumbs up. "It's good to be here."

Since my return to campus not everyone had been friendly. Though more kids had been supportive than I'd expected.

I got a few looks in the elevator ride up. Of course, Vi had to live on the top floor—gave me plenty of time to stare at the numbers as they lit up above the doors.

When I stepped out, I pulled my cap's brim low, shading my eyes. As I made my way along the corridor, I didn't miss the feminine gasps as I passed doors—as well as the tunes and hums from hairdryers.

"What's *he* doing here?" sniped a voice from behind.

I bristled but pretended not to notice. Best thing was to ignore her and anyone else who decided to comment.

Stopping at 914, I glanced over my shoulder. Three females stood in the hall watching me. Two gaped like Will Smith had just sauntered past, another just crossed her arms and scowled. I waved and tried to smile. "Good evening, ladies."

Yes, I sounded totally lame.

To their snorts and giggles, I turned and knocked. At least the chicks behind weren't running for the exit and screaming for the police. If only I were a hermit living in the locker room, I'd be spared from the looks, the comments, even the praise. Sure, I'd enjoyed the attention before. But now I wished I were invisible.

No one liked to have their sex life scrutinized under a microscope, nonetheless in front of a jury. God, I never wanted to go through that again.

The door opened in about two seconds, but I barely recognized the Amazon on the other side.

"Whoa," I said, my jaw dropping to my chest. God save me, Vivian had morphed from nerdy accountant into... Hell, with her hair styled in long shiny waves, she looked like dynamite—like one of the girls I was trying to stay away from.

"Crap!" She crossed her arms over her cleavage—I mean a really perfect rack, boobs I wouldn't be able to ignore for more than five seconds. "I knew this was a disaster."

As soon as the words left her lips, the door slammed in my face.

Stunned, I stared straight ahead. How many girls were standing in the hallway now? I grunted, imagining tomorrow's headlines, *"Williams Stood Up by Tutor."*

Shit.

About to turn and suffer the walk of shame down the corridor, the door opened and a blonde girl popped her head out. "Sorry, Vi's changing. And don't get the wrong impression, dude. The makeover was my idea."

I tried to peer through the crack above blonde-girl's head but saw nothing except the shirt Vivian had been wearing sailing through the air. "No prob," I said. "You must be the pre-law major who's been rooming with Vi since freshman year." I stuck out my hand. "I'm Cade."

She checked over her shoulder, then opened the door a bit further and gripped my palm like she was attempting to crush a walnut. "Lisa, nice to meet you...I think."

I pulled my hand away and splayed my fingers. "Why *think*?"

She looked me up and down like a cross-examining attorney, instantly turning my stomach sour. "To begin with, you asked her to a footballer's party after your first tutoring session." Lisa poked me in the chest with her pointer finger. Hard. "And I'll have you know she's a nice girl—not one of those whorific floozes. Not even close."

Trying not to snort, I swiped a hand over my mouth. *Whorific floozes*? I didn't expect urban slang to come from a pre-law senior. "Um...that's why I thought she'd be a good friend to take to this party."

"I'm ready!" Vi smiled, pulling open the door, smoothing her hands down a purple sleeveless turtleneck—no cleavage, but snug-fitting and still more to look at than I needed. At least her hair had been tousled when she changed but, if you ask me, it was even sexier that way. "Sorry. I borrowed Lisa's shirt but as soon as I opened the door and saw your face I knew it was a total disaster."

My opinion? She was kinda right. I would have had too much trouble keeping my hands to myself.

"Maybe it was too much," said the roommate, grabbing my wrist and giving me one of those "Mom knows best" expressions. "Have her home at a decent hour. It's a school night, you know."

Not wanting another cross-examination, I gently twisted my hand away and grinned. "I'll let Vi decide what's best."

Miss Unbelievably-Gorgeous pulled the door shut. "Bye, Lisa."

After we made it to the elevator bank, I pushed the button, leaned in, and asked, "Does your roomie often dress you?" Holy hell, she smelled like the Caribbean, coconuts and lime, and *sex*. I gulped.

No.

Definitely not sex.

Vi groaned, dropping her head back and blushing. "Only when I'm about to be thrown to the wolves."

"Wolves?"

"You know, dragged into a party with hormones bouncing off the walls."

"Which is why Lisa chose the—" I drew an arc across my chest. "The lowcut shirt?" It just didn't make sense.

"I know. It was over the top. But she said if I was serious about being chick repellent then I needed to look the part. But after I put the shirt on, I thought..." Vi bit her lip when the elevator arrived.

I led her inside and punched the ground floor button. "What did you think?"

"It made me feel vulnerable."

My chest hurt like she'd just issued a jab to my heart. Because of me? Because of my reputation? "Oh."

"No!" She window-washered both hands. "Not because of you but because there was too much of *me* on display. It just didn't feel right."

The pain vanished. "Good."

"Good?" she asked as the G lit up and the doors opened.

"Yeah," I said, leading her out through the foyer while I dropped the pass in front of the dude at the desk. "You okay with walking? Devan's apartment is across campus."

"Seriously?" Vi jammed her fists into her hips, making her shoulders throw back and her breasts far too unignorable. I think she was attempting to be assertive, but she only managed to make my knees go weak. "I walk everywhere. Or take the bus."

I ran my hand down my mouth, erasing my grin but totally unable to forget her hotness. "No car, huh?"

"With my tuition? I doubt I'll be able to afford a car before I'm fifty."

I chuckled.

"I mean it," she said with an edge to her voice. "You might have a free ride, but mine's far from it."

I guess she did have some preconceived ideas about me. I didn't say anything for a while. A few weeks ago, I faced the very real possibility of paying my own tuition—if I ever managed to be accepted to another college. My thoughts bounced around and kept coming back to her. I wanted to tell her she looked nice, but that would sound lame, wouldn't it?

Yeah, I'm the stud on campus.

Not.

About halfway to Devan's I stopped as the audible alarm at a pedestrian crossing beeped and a car zoomed by. But Vi kept going like she was on a mission.

"Whoa!" Grabbing her wrist, I yanked her back to the curb.

"Ack!" she squealed as she stumbled into me.

Reacting, my hands wrapped around her waist, pulling her into my chest to ensure she wouldn't fall. "You okay?" I asked as a crackle of hot energy pulsed through my entire body. Holy mother, she felt good. An unintended moan rumbled in my throat.

I stood totally stunned for a second. Jeez, I hadn't been this close to a woman since...

Immediately, Vi planted her palms on my chest while she blushed scarlet. "Sorry. I guess I'm a klutz today. Good thing I didn't wear heels."

Reluctantly, I stepped away, keeping hold of her shoulders. "You walk *everywhere*?" I asked, trying to sound like I was teasing. Anything not to betray the way my heart was pounding right now.

Staring at my chest, Vi snapped her fingers away. "I-I guess I wasn't paying attention."

I raised her chin with the crook of my finger. Without her glasses, her eyes shone like polished mahogany. "That doesn't seem like you." I mean she'd pulled the badass, take-charge tutor thing yesterday. My guess was there wasn't much that slipped past her.

"No. Sorry."

"You don't need to keep apologizing." When the light changed, I took her hand and led her across the street. Though she was a good-sized woman, her hand seemed incredibly small in mine. I hadn't realized how fine-boned she was. Man, she had soft skin, too. "We're both nervous."

Vi nudged me with her elbow. "You may be nervous but at least you can manage to avoid nearly being run over."

She didn't let go of my hand either. Weird, but it felt kinda comfortable as if I were holding hands with someone special. Hell, Vi was special. I mean, how many bookworms would agree to pose as my date just to keep girls from coming on to me?

But she had.

Now, if she managed to avoid falling into me again, I ought to be able to get through the night without doing something stupid. Like kissing my tutor.

Crossing over to the apartment building, I released her hand, swiped my card, and opened the glass door. "This is it."

"Do you live here, too?"

"Yeah. A lot of the juniors and seniors on the team do." I bit my lip, not wanting to tell her each of us had our own apartment, especially after picking her up at the dorm and learning that she took the bus. She was right about the players getting a free ride, but she probably didn't know we put our asses on the line every gameday. Some practices, too. Bottom line, the school made millions off our sweat.

"It's nice," she said as we rode yet another elevator up to the top floor. The starting quarterback, Devan, scored the "penthouse" which meant he had an extra bathroom and about a measly hundred square feet more than the rest of us.

An awkward silence hung in the air as I watched Vivian out of the corner of my eye. She fidgeted with her hair, winding a strand around her finger. She didn't need to worry. I had it all planned. We'd say hi, smile a lot, and stay long enough to drink something non-alcoholic.

As the elevator opened, *Holiday* rocked the floor.

"Let me guess," she said. "The prize is behind the door with the loud music."

"You're not into Green Day?"

She headed for Devan's apartment—no need to tell her we'd just passed mine. We wouldn't be stopping there anyway. "I didn't say that."

I fell in step beside her. "So you like them?"

"Mm hmm. Went to their concert last year. Did you?"

My jaw twitched. Green Day was not the only thing I'd missed. "Wasn't here."

"God." She stopped and folded her arms across her midriff. Damn, would she stop striking poses that accentuated how amazing her tits were? "Sorry. I'm such an idiot."

"No, you're not." I leaned against the wall beside her and wiped my eyes. "Are you nervous?"

"No," she clipped, looking away.

I scratched my head under my ball cap. "Well, I am."

"Wait. You?"

"Sure. That's why I wanted you with me."

"Aren't these guys your friends?"

"They are but…"

A single, delicate eyebrow arched. "Tell me."

Rubbing the back of my neck, I groaned like I was in the hall being reprimanded by my sixth-grade teacher. "Do you have any idea how difficult it is to come back to Madison?"

"I'm sure it must be weird, but didn't the news say your teammates all supported you?"

"Thank God. It's the only thing that made my return bearable."

She dropped her arms to her sides. "Um, then you're seriously nervous about partying with girls?"

My secret was out. "I don't want them thinking I'm an easy mark. I don't want them looking at me like I'm some sort of porn star—or worse, some sexual predator. I swore when I came back I'd put my social life on hold and focus on two things—football and grades."

"Wow. I'm impressed." She tugged my hand and inclined her head toward the door. "So, let's do this thing and show 'em you mean business."

I grinned, liking Vi a little more. Except as soon as we walked into the apartment, both Devan and Jason deposited themselves either side of her.

Jason jabbed me in the shoulder. "Yo, Willie," he whispered in my ear. "You didn't tell me your tutor was a hottie."

That's because I didn't realize exactly how hot she was until I picked her up. Still, the hair on the back of my neck bristled. He might be my best friend, but sometimes Jason had a way of making me want to bury my knuckles in his face. I ushered him aside. "Give the woman some room."

Devan raised his glass. "I have a room down the hall, sweetheart."

Vi looped her arm through mine and squeezed. "And there's no way in hell I'd be interested in seeing it, dude."

Devan licked his finger and drilled it into his ass, making a hissing noise. "Whoa, talk dirty to me, babe."

I gave him a stink eye as well. The two drooling stags followed as we moved further inside. I introduced her to some of the guys and a few of the girls I knew.

I grabbed a sports drink. "Want one or something stronger?"

"Are you having that?"

"Yep. Practice is at six a.m."

"This is perfect." She took the bottle and twisted off the cap. "I thought you'd be drinking beer."

"No way. My two priorities, remember?"

Grinning, she took a sip. "You're full of surprises."

Jason sidled up beside Vi and grabbed her elbow. "Want to dance?"

She gave him a seriously badass stare. "I don't think so."

The dude didn't flinch. He just took her power drink and handed it to me. "Sorry, Vivian, but rookies aren't allowed to say no."

Chapter Six

Vivian

Cade disappeared from view as his friend pulled me through the crowd. Jason had to be at least six-two. I'd never been anywhere with so many guys who towered over me. Heck, *I* usually towered over everyone, not the other way around.

"So, you're an accounting major?" he shouted above the music as we moved closer to the micro-speakers.

"Uh huh."

He planted his hands on my hips and started moving, making me swing with him. Except we were the only ones dancing. I rarely ever danced, let alone made a spectacle of myself.

"This is awkward," I shouted as my elbow bumped a guy in the back. "Sorry!"

The dude glanced over his shoulder with a scowl, but when he spotted Jason he moved on.

"I really should find Cade." I cupped a hand to my mouth. "After all, I'm his..." I couldn't bring myself to say "date" and "tutor" sounded too lame.

"Don't worry about it, Willie can handle himself."

Right, and that's why he asked me to tag along. I glanced around the room. Sure thing, just about every girl I saw was wearing a skimpy halter top like the one I'd borrowed from Lisa. "But isn't this party for him?"

"Sure is."

The music changed to a Beyoncé tune and suddenly the living room was packed with gyrating bodies. Stretching up on my toes, I caught a glimpse of the kitchen.

"Cripes!" I swore, twisting my hips from Jason's grasp. "Sorry, but duty calls."

"Huh?" His voice resounded over the thundering drums.

I marched toward Cade with my fists clenched. Just like he'd said, some dynamite blonde pressed her body against him, her lips practically nuzzling his neck.

I pushed between them, making the girl stumble backward on her six-inch heels. "Hey!" she shrieked.

"See what happens when the number one wide receiver asks me to dance?" I asked as the blonde huffed and started away. I raised my voice. "Some hussy moves in on my man. You're blocking for me, aren't you, sweetheart?"

God, I couldn't believe I just said that. Thank goodness Lisa had given me a few pointers. I'd learned that at tight end Williams caught short passes and blocked for the quarterback while Jason didn't do as much blocking and caught more passes—especially the long ones.

Cade's eyes lit up as I possessively wrapped my hands around his arm. "I didn't think you followed football."

In the interest of putting on a good show, I smoothed my fingers up and down his bicep. Good Lord, he had to have the most well-muscled arm I'd ever touched in my life. Yesterday when he'd removed his hoodie, it certainly was the most well-muscled arm I'd ever *seen*. Pecs, too. Of course, I shouldn't admit his ass was eye candy.

No.

Definitely not. Gah, talk about a tutor/student breach.

"I'm a quick study," I said, retrieving my sports drink and guzzling. Maybe I should have asked for something stronger. But then, again, there was no way on earth I was going to get tipsy here. Not with Cade, and not with all these ripped football players. Every dude in this apartment was a chick magnet.

Screwing the cap back on, I closed my eyes.

I'm only here because I'm helping my student focus on his objective of improving his grades. I will not fixate on another tight ass, nor will I ogle anyone's pecs, biceps, abs, and that includes those of the man with whom I have an appointment.

Cade brushed my cheek, making sparks fly, I was sure of it. Did the dude have Superman powers on top of everything else? "Are you okay?" he asked.

I opened my eyes, only to stare at his smile—straight, beautiful, white teeth. He must have worn braces. "Uh huh," I squeaked. "The question is are you?"

"Yeah, and thanks for the rescue."

"Why do you let them glom onto you like that?"

"I shouldn't, I guess. It's just I don't like being rude."

"Oh yeah, like invading your personal space isn't rude." I glanced down to my hand gripping his arm, noticing the side of my breast pushing into it as well. I immediately released him and took a step away. "Sorry. I was merely playing bodyguard."

"You mean chick repellant?"

I laughed. "Something like that."

"Well, you don't have to apologize for being an ace."

My stomach levitated as if I'd just downed a glass of champagne. "I did good, huh?"

Slinging his arm across my shoulders, he gave me a side-squeeze. "Yeah, teach."

That's right, just keep reminding me that I'm your tutor.

The music cut off.

"Ladies and gentlemen," Jason boomed, waving his hands. "I'd like to take a moment to welcome the baddest tight end Madison has ever laid eyes upon, our brother in the huddle, a man among men, Cade Williams!"

I clapped and cheered along with everyone else while Devan came from a back room carrying a football-shaped cake and set it on the kitchen counter beside the man of the moment.

"*Brothers stand together, welcome back, Willie,*" Cade read the icing inscription across the ball. "Wow, this means a lot."

I knew it struck deep because his eyes glossed over.

Jason slid his elbows onto the counter, looking smug. "I wanted to add number two in receiving yards, but there wasn't enough room."

Cade brandished a knife. "That's because the cake's not for *you*, bro."

The crowd hooted, though Jason wasn't laughing.

"So, Cade," said the girl who'd been flirting with him. "You can play catch with me any time."

I was about to object when Devan did it for me, "Give it a rest, Piper. Can't you see he's off the market?"

"What? With the towering blubber girl?"

Cade stopped cutting cake and slowly set down the knife. "I call foul." He threw his thumb over his shoulder. "Ejected for taunting."

"Hey." Jason held up his hands. "Don't listen to her, she's plastered."

"That's the problem. But thanks for the cake. I really appreciate everything you've done to make me feel part of the team. You guys are the best friends I've ever had, but I'm just not ready to party." He grabbed my hand and pulled me toward the door, turning his lips toward my ear and whispering, "Sorry. You didn't come here to be insulted."

I sure didn't. *Blubber girl?* I was into high fitness and yoga four times a week and I walked everywhere. Sure, I had curves, but blubber?

Absolutely not.

Neither of us said a word on the elevator ride down.

But when the doors opened, Cade didn't budge. "I like your...um...figure. And don't let any flat-assed, blind-drunk bitch tell you differently, okay?"

The doors closed. "Thanks." As we started up to some unknown floor, I punched the G. "But I'd just as soon not go back up there."

"Yeah. Sorry." He took off his cap and raked his fingers through his incredibly thick dark-brown hair. He'd had a hat on for hours and he still looked amazing. "I think I need food. Not cake. You hungry?"

My stomach growled on cue. "There's no need to feed me."

"No need?" He eyed the source of the growl. "After your performance tonight? The least I can do is buy you a burger."

"I really shouldn't," I said just as my tummy protested again.

Cade arched an eyebrow, adding bubbles to my hunger pangs. "Hey, the complaints from your stomach are rattling the walls. A clear indication that you need to eat."

"Busted." I licked my lips. What harm was there in grabbing a bite? "Lisa's makeover made me miss dinner."

"I know just he place." He punched the button for the parking garage. "You ever been on a Harley before?"

Chapter Seven

Vivian

"Ugh, I have helmet hair," I groaned, snagging my fingers in my rat's nest as Cade led me toward a dive bar with a partly-lit neon sign that read "Cruisers".

"It looks great." He held the door for me. "Windblown."

I gave him a pointed glance of disbelief as I strode through. Rather than chuckle or wink or do anything to hint that he was teasing, he just smiled, his pale blue eyes intently focused on my face as if he had never told a lie in his life.

Maybe he did like wild hair.

And why should I care?

The problem?

I did care and somehow I needed to stop.

Tonight.

Inside, the smell of a hot grill made my mouth water. It was a typical Wisconsin hole-in-the-wall. I'd lived around these places all my life. In fact, when Cade had started heading north, I'd thought he might take the interstate leading to Mom's. But then, he had no idea where Mom lived.

"Hey, dude," said the guy behind the bar, pointing with a rag in his hand. "Your booth's open."

"Thanks." Cade put his hand in the small of my back. "You okay with a burger?"

I didn't see any menus, not even a chalk board. "Sounds good."

"Two specials," he said as he led me past a couple of diners and two guys on stools watching a baseball game.

He gestured to a booth large enough to fit a family of eight and slid in across from me.

"You must be popular around here to have your own booth."

"Nah, all the guys come here especially when..." His gaze shifted away.

"When?" I pressed.

He punched the worn, red vinyl seat. "When we want some quiet, like after a loss."

I bit my lip. He'd probably been there a few times during trial. Poor guy. I still couldn't imagine what he'd been through.

Leaning forward on his elbows, Cade's expression softened. "Have you been to the town of Windsor before?"

"Not that I know of." I glanced around—signed pictures of football players, metal craft beer signs, a wooden black-and-white dairy cow. I checked over the bar for a cheese head and wasn't disappointed. Since the town wasn't on the interstate corridor, I probably hadn't been here with Mom or Grandpa. "Aren't you from New Jersey?"

"Yep."

"How did you find this place?"

Cade passed a saltshaker between his fingers, the glass container shifting as fast as blinking lights. "The seniors bring the incoming freshmen here for Olympus Burgers."

"Olympus?"

"Yeah, they're a foot high and anyone who doesn't eat theirs has to wear a baby bib to practices for the rest of the year."

"I'd lose for sure." I eyed him. "But I'll bet you didn't."

"Nah, I'm not a bib man, myself."

I glanced toward the door to the kitchen and the sizzling coming from beyond. "You didn't order Olympus Burgers for us did you?"

"The specials just have the works."

I knew what that meant...hamburger, cheese, egg, bacon, fried onions.

He set the saltshaker aside. "Besides, I'm pretty sure they don't have salad here."

"What makes you think I eat salad?"

"Don't all girls?"

Those light blue eyes met mine, making me press my palms against my somersaulting stomach. "Well, I do eat salad, but I'm not fixated on counting calories." Gah, I was hungry, not giddy. The food couldn't come fast enough.

"Awesome."

I wondered if all the girls he'd dated were toothpicks. Probably. But I'd been brought up around restaurants and when it came right down to it, I loved food. Sure, I tried to stick to a healthy diet for the most part but grabbing a works burger now and again wasn't going to kill me. I'd just exercise a bit harder at the gym tomorrow. Maybe run between classes as well.

The barman brought over a pitcher of water and two glasses. "You want anything else to drink?"

Cade looked my way and arched his eyebrows.

"Not for me, thanks." I picked up the pitcher and poured for us both. "No beer?"

He raised his glass. "Six a.m. practice, remember? Anyway, I'm driving."

I laughed. "A Harley."

"Hey, I worked a lot of hours to buy that bike."

"It's nice, but totally impractical for Wisconsin winters."

Blowing a raspberry, Cade's shoulders fell. "I know. To be honest, I've been thinking about trading it in."

"What do you usually do in the winter?"

"Bum rides, borrow Jason's car." He flashed a grin sexy enough to make goosebumps shoot down my arms. "But there's nothing that compares to the smooth ride from Jersey."

I rubbed my arms. "You drove that thing halfway across the country?"

"Better than flying."

"Seriously? But flying is so much faster."

"Sure, it's faster. It's just not cruising."

The burgers came and I turned my head sideways for a good look at the pile of food the bartender planted in front of me. "Are you sure this isn't Mount Olympus?"

Cade popped a fry in his mouth. "Positive. Believe me. *You'd* be eating an Olympus for a week."

I grabbed the special with both hands, opened my mouth as wide as I could, and gave it my best effort.

Watching my every move, Cade snorted. "I dare you to finish it."

"I definitely do not accept." I pulled a napkin from the dispenser and wiped the sauce from the corners of my lips. "I don't take dares from my students."

The air grew a bit charged with my last comment, but I'd said it to keep things real.

Turning my attention to my food, I watched Cade through lowered eyelashes. He was much better at biting the whole burger than I'd been. Better at keeping the sauce off his face, too.

"Why did you come back to Madison?" I blurted before I thought. "Couldn't you go anywhere you wanted?"

He looked up, slowly lowering his hands to his plate. I could tell by the knit of his eyebrows the question bothered him. "It's complicated. But in a nutshell, if I'd transferred to another school I might have had to sit out a year because of eligibility. Plus, my attorney said..."

I moved to the edge of the seat. "What?"

"It doesn't matter. Let's just say I had the best chance of picking up the pieces of my life if I returned like nothing happened."

"It had to be hard."

He looked at me while a dark shadow crossed his face, speaking a thousand words. I took in a shaky inhale as, within a glimpse, I understood the depth of his pain. Returning to Madison had to be the hardest thing he'd ever done in his life—maybe even harder than being accused of sexual assault and fighting to prove his innocence.

Unable to hold his gaze, I dropped my eyes to my hands.

God, now that I'd spent some time with Cade, the whole bad boy reputation didn't fit.

He wasn't the type.

Honestly, he was kind of a gentleman, at least as gentlemanly as dudes came these days.

Wondering what had really happened and knowing there was no way in hell I was going to ask, I took another bite of my burger as he licked his fingers, his plate completely empty.

He swiped one of my fries. "Enough about me. What about you? Where're you from?"

I gulped down a swig of water. "A tiny town between Madison and Milwaukee called Johnson Creek."

"That can't be far."

"About an hour and a half on the bus."

"You go home much?"

"Some," I said, not wanting to tell him Mom worked most weekends because the tips were better. I mean, not many students at Madison had moms who were waitresses.

"Do you have any brothers and sisters?"

"Just me."

I'd been asked that question a million times but it always made a chill pulse through my blood. To this day I wondered what I could have done differently to convince Dad to stay. But he'd never given me the opportunity to ask.

"How about you?" I drummed my fingers. "Do you have siblings?"

"Two younger sisters. Twins. They're both still in high school."

I pursed my lips to hold in questions I knew I shouldn't ask. How did his family handle his arrest? Did the girls face problems at school? "I'll bet they're total knockouts."

Cade rolled his eyes to the ceiling. "Tell me about it."

I watched him eat my fries. Here we sat, two people who had zilch in common. Yet I was drawn to him, not only because he was drop-dead gorgeous but because I sensed he was the most misunderstood person in the entire student body.

Cade held so much inside. I guess I did, too. But my problems seemed so insignificant compared to his.

My phone lit up with a text from Lisa.

RU OK? Thought u'd be home by now.

Jeez, it was only nine-forty-five.

I'm Gr8. Be there soon.

Cade watched my thumbs tap the keyboard.

I clicked the screen off. "That was Lisa checking in."

"She worried about you?"

"Always."

"I guess I can't blame her...especially when you're out with someone like me."

"Bull," I said sliding out of the booth. "Anyone who thinks that doesn't know you."

Chapter Eight

Cade

"The balance sheet represents assets and liabilities while the profit and loss statement reflects income and expense," Vi explained for the third time as if repeating herself would help it sink in. She continued on in more detail describing how payments and receipts would be allocated to different accounts based on the reason for the income or expense.

I blankly stared at the list of items to be allocated to the plethora of accounts she'd rattled off. Until something clicked. "Wait."

Stopping mid-sentence, she shifted her attention from the worksheet to my face. God those brown eyes could make any man melt. My heart flew to my throat. For the fifth time today I didn't move. I didn't even blink until my mind engaged again.

Coughing, I tapped my finger on the screen of her laptop. "The balance sheet is defense and the profit and loss is the offense."

Taking in a deep breath, she started to say something but shook her head instead. Now it was her turn to be knocked out of her zone. "Sorry, but I don't follow."

"You really don't know *anything* about football?"

She cringed, slowly shaking her head. "No one ever watched it when I was growing up."

"Not even your dad?"

"I don't know if he did or not."

"Oh."

Shit. I'd asked her where she was from, but she never got around to talking about her parents. Hell, plenty of girls didn't watch football. I shouldn't be surprised.

Maybe a little disappointed.

"Well," I said. "The defense doesn't score all that often because their job is to prevent the other team from scoring. If you have a good defense it is an asset to the team, but if they suck, it's a liability."

"Interesting."

"I reckon the offense is the P and L because that's where the team wins or loses. If they score more field goals and touchdowns than the other team, it's a win—a profit in my books because the team and the school bring in more money especially if they have a winning season and they get to go to the playoffs and a bowl game. No lie, that's big bucks, baby."

Vi sat back, clicking her pen. "Wow, that's astonishing. I never would have thought to make a sports analogy in an accounting lesson."

"Well, it wouldn't come to you if you weren't a fan. I mean, I study and I go to practice, and—"

Her nostrils flared. "You party."

I sliced my hand through the air. "I *used* to party." I opened the front of my notebook and tapped it. "Remember? My two goals—they're right here. I look at them at the beginning of every class, every study session."

She leaned in, pointing to the top. "As you told me, football is first."

"Absolutely."

She crossed her arms and pursed her lips. "Hmm."

"You sound skeptical."

"Well, before I met you I thought football was just a bunch of bullies pushing each other around."

I gave her a good look from head to toe. Had I won her over? "You thought? What changed your mind?"

"I suppose it hasn't completely changed, but *you've* surprised me."

"How?"

"I don't know." Vi started packing up as if she were busying herself to avoid looking directly at me. "When I found out I'd be your tutor, I expected an attitude."

A year ago, she probably would have gotten a major one.

"But what's the draw? Why is football so important?" she asked. "Is it all about money?"

"Hey, I'm a college ball player. I may be on scholarship, but I'm poor. You should see my bank account. It has way more debits than credits."

"I'm sure it's healthier than mine." She slid her pen into the front pocket of her backpack and stood. "I still don't understand. Don't you worry about getting hurt? I mean, seriously hurt?"

"Yeah, and that's why my butt is in this chair and my attitude is focused. Because there aren't any guarantees. I might have been a cocky freshman and sophomore, but last year was..." *Unbearable, sickening, crushing.*

"Go on."

I didn't want to relive it. Not ever. "It was like being knocked out and waking up in hell."

She hissed through her teeth as if she could feel my pain. "God, I'm sorry."

"So am I."

"It's amazing that you were strong enough to come back," she said, giving me a sad smile and starting for the door.

I hopped up and blocked her path. I needed to explain. I wasn't a bully. Sure, it got rough on the field, but as soon as the whistle blew it was over and time to focus on the next play. "Football has been a part of my life as far back as I can remember. Getting the call to come to Madison was the best day of my life. I was full of hope. My dad was so proud I don't think he stopped grinning for a week."

Leaning against the door, Vi smiled. "I'll bet he was."

Her smile made me feel like I was floating, though what I was about to say was about to make a lead ball drop to the bottom of my gut.

Hers, too.

I clenched my fists. To make her truly understand how much my two goals meant, I had to tell her. "But my dad never saw me play college ball."

With a gasp, she covered her mouth. "Oh my God. What—"

"Happened?"

She nodded, her eyes misting as if she already knew.

Resting my hand on the wall beside her ear, I swallowed while that lead ball slowly sank. "He stopped at a convenience store to buy some milk and walked in at the wrong time. The place was being robbed and Dad tried to step in." I sucked in a breath through clenched teeth. "The coward shot him."

"No," she whispered while a tear dribbled from her eye. "How awful and then you..."

I knew what she was going to say and I was glad she didn't. "Some people are dealt tougher hands than others. But that's not why I told you about my father."

"Oh?"

"Don't get me wrong, I love football with every fiber of my body, but I've made it my life's quest to make him proud. To be the man Dad wanted me to be. He believed in me. He was my coach from peewee through high school. He gave me strength and I am absolutely positive his strength is what helped me keep it together during the trial."

By the time I shut my mouth I was shaking. I'd never said any of this out loud, not to anyone.

Dropping her backpack, Vi reached for me.

Pulled me into her arms.

Pulled me into her soft body.

And God forgive me, I wanted to stay there all night. I wanted to bawl my eyes out and bare my soul.

"I'm so sorry," she whispered, her arms enveloping me, cradling me in more comfort than I deserved. "I wish I had the words."

I moved my hands to hug her back.

But I stopped, my heart twisting into a hundred knots.

God, she smelled so good.

Felt so good.

And yet I stood there, my body stiff as an iron rod.

I was petrified.

In a blink she dropped her arms and backed away, picked up her backpack, and pushed out the door. Turning, she gave me a sad smile. "For what it's worth, I'm glad you're here and I'll do everything I can to help you with goal number two."

Chapter Nine

Vivian

Cripes!

I hugged him.

And he didn't hug me back!

What the hell was I thinking?

I'll never forget the look on his face. It was as if he were mortified.

Gah!

That had to be the most awkward moment of my life. The stupidest thing I'd ever done.

Marching toward the library door, I was so pissed with myself I didn't see the crowd until I was outside.

"It's her!" someone shouted as the mob surrounded me.

"Leave me alone," I sniped, as I shrugged into my backpack.

"Is it true you're Cade William's tutor?"

"What is he studying?"

"Is he failing?"

I waved my hands in front of my face. "Would you people give it a rest?"

"Is he behaving himself?"

The back of my neck burned as my gaze snapped to the idiot. "What kind of question is that?"

"You're Vivian Ellis, aren't you?"

How the heck did they know?

"I might be," I replied as the door whooshed open behind me. "But it doesn't give you the right to mob a student as she's leaving the—"

"Step away and give her some room," boomed Cade, his voice menacing as he moved beside me, placing his palm in the small of my back. "Leave Vi alone. If you want to razz someone, you'd better come after me."

In a split second a gazillion thoughts raced through my mind. I wanted to run but didn't at the same time. He challenged them? He was the last person on the planet who needed more harassment. These vultures ought to lay off—like yesterday.

"A-and Cade needs to study," I stammered, standing taller. "You have no right to badger him on campus."

I didn't have a clue if they could harass him or not, but it sounded good.

"One important question," said a man at the rear.

Cade stared him down while I scooted a little closer to my student.

"Will you be starting in Saturday's game?"

"All I can say is I'm ready. You want to know more, I'll see you on the Gyrfalcon field at noon. Until then I have no comment." His hand pressed against my back as we headed straight through the crowd. "Later dudes."

"Later?" I whispered as we broke through. "Can we do that?"

"We just did, didn't we?"

"But they were totally out of line. I can't believe you didn't chew them out."

Or clobber someone.

He smirked. "Getting pissed makes the team look bad. Players always have to take the high road."

My hands shook as I glanced over my shoulder. "How can you stand them?"

"It happens." He kept going, taking the turn to Prentiss Hall. "But it's annoying especially since the trial. I'm hoping the jerks will back off once the season starts and there're more important things to report."

My blood was still boiling. "Saturday can't come soon enough."

"Amen."

"Don't you ever want to deck somebody?"

"You're kidding." He stopped outside the dorm and swept my hair away from my face. I couldn't imagine how difficult it must be for him to always keep his cool. "They'd crucify me."

My cheek tingled where his fingers had brushed the skin. Absently, I placed my hand over the spot to stop the sensation. "Well, we don't need that kind of attention ever again. I'll talk to Professor Lumsden first thing tomorrow morning. There ought to be a study room in the accounting department we can use. Obviously, the library is too public."

The big tight end gave a thumb's up. "Good idea. You think he'll have a place?"

"Probably." I shuffled toward the door. "I mean, the School of Business has its own building. There ought to be a spare office or something."

Cade followed me into the foyer. "So, you coming to Saturday's game?"

With a ding, the elevator arrived and I jumped in. "I don't have tickets," I said right before the doors closed.

Chapter Ten

Vivian

It figured. I'd spent so much time focusing on tutoring, on Friday night I was up to my eyeballs in homework when my phone dinged with a text.

My heart jolted. I usually got a jolt when my phone sounded unexpectedly, but this time it was like an electrical zing—except it felt good. Maybe because the text was from Cade.

"Hey Teach. Check your e-mail."

I sort of half laughed, half gasped. After all, he hadn't asked me to be chick repellent since the first date...I mean first *appointment*. Of course, the party was not a date and we still definitely were not dating.

Absolutely not.

The idea of dating hadn't even crossed my mind.

And I wouldn't admit if it had.

Not even to myself.

"What?" Lisa asked, lowering her novel.

I shrugged and batted a hand through the air as if my stomach hadn't practically leapt across the room. "Just a text from Cade."

"Oh, really?" She slid off her bed and sauntered toward me. "So he's texting you now?"

"Not usually. He asked me to check my e-mail. It's probably an assignment he wants me to review before he submits it." I slid my finger across the touchpad on my laptop and tapped. Sure enough, I had a new e-mail but it wasn't from Cade. It was from the Madison Alumni Association.

"Well?"

I opened it. "Oh wow. He sent two tickets to the game."

"Let me see." She shoved her butt beside mine and took over my computer. "Holy shit. These aren't in the student section either."

I nudged her aside enough to see the screen. "Where are they? The parking lot?"

"Huh uh, girl. These are on the fifty-yard line right behind the Gyrfalcon bench. Best seats in the house if you ask me."

I grabbed the computer and plopped it back on my lap. "No way."

"I wonder if those are family seats."

"Might be," I said as I brought up the stadium seating map. Good Lord, Lisa was right. "His mom lives in New Jersey."

"Are you gonna go?"

"Will you go with me?"

"You don't have to ask me twice."

"Even though you don't like football?" I snorted. After she gave me the crash course on football terms I was guessing Lisa liked the game more than she let on.

My roomie smacked her lips. "Mmm. I think I ought to pay attention this year."

"Grad student?"

"Sexy PhD student who's teaching my corporate law class."

"Sounds intriguing," I said, picking up my phone. "What's he like?"

"At the moment he practically doesn't know I exist. But yesterday he was wearing Devan Thomas's jersey so I asked if he was going to the game."

"What did he say?"

Lisa shimmied her shoulders. "That he hasn't missed a game since freshman year."

"And you think he'll notice you're at a game in an arena with..." I checked my screen. "Eighty thousand people?"

"He might not see me there, but I'll have plenty of fodder for conversation on Monday."

I had to laugh. Lisa never had trouble coming up with conversation. It was inherent to being a pre-law major.

Shaking my head, I fired off a text to Cade.

"You're hell bent on getting me to a game, aren't you?"

"You're not a little curious?"

"Bullies, remember?"

"I thought you were over that."

"Change is difficult for me."

"So...you'll be there?"

I stared up at the ceiling, trying to come up with a witty reply, then typed, *"I do happen to have that exact time open on my inordinately busy schedule."*

"!!"

I giggled, my stomach flipping at the exclamation points.

Of course, they weren't just any exclamation points.

Cade had typed them.

Lisa grabbed my phone. "You sound like a teenage girl going gaga."

I snatched it back. "I'm not finished."

My thumbs flew over the keys. *"Hey, thanks. Lisa's psyched."*

"Cool. Tell her hi."

I set the phone on my right side, away from my nosy roommate. "Cade says hi."

"To me?"

"Yes, to you."

"Oh." She leaned against Aquaman and crossed her arms. "Did you thank him for the tickets?"

"Uh huh."

She drummed the tips of her fingers together. "Soooooo, exactly what has happened since you went to that stupid party with him?"

Eyes wide, I affected my most unflappable expression. "Nothing."

"Seriously?" She smacked me with the pillow. "No, girl. There have been far too many giggles and gasps coming from this corner of the room. I need the facts."

After the party I'd been pretty sketchy about everything except for saying that Cade had definitely needed chick repellant. I conveniently forgot to tell her about riding on his Harley and having a burger at Cruisers. That was immaterial in my mind. After all, I didn't want Lisa to think we were dating. Or had a chance at a relationship. Honestly, I didn't want anyone to think we were dating.

Because we weren't.

Jeez, after he told me about his dad I'd hugged him. Not because I had the hots for him, but because I felt it was the right thing to do. But he'd turned to ice in my arms. God, how totally awkward, not to mention embarrassing.

"He likes you," she blurted as if we really were back in high school.

Good Lord, if only my stomach would stop with the butterflies. Worse, my cheeks suddenly felt like Lisa was holding a torch to them. And she noticed everything.

Shaking my head, I hid my blush under my palms. "No, no, no. He absolutely does not *like-like* me. Yesterday he used a football analogy to understand the fundamentals of accounting. I'm sure he just wants me to become familiar with where he's coming from. You know, so we'll sort of speak the same language."

Chapter Eleven

Cade

As soon as we ran out onto the field for warmups, my gaze shot directly to Vi's seats—the same place Mom sat when she came to town.

A rock sank in my gut.

She wasn't there. But then, fans were still filing in.

I tried not to look again as the captain led us through our routine. I didn't steal another glimpse until I trotted over to join the receivers. Damn, the seats were still vacant.

Had something happened?

Was she okay? Did she suddenly come down with the flu? Had reporters mobbed her outside the stadium?

"Williams!" shouted Coach.

Realizing it was my turn, I ran a wheel route, but just as I turned the ball hit me in the helmet.

Some of the crowd laughed.

Coach marched toward me. "Where the hell were you looking?"

Dammit, this was game day and I needed to stop worrying about my tutor. She said she'd come and if she didn't it wasn't any skin off my nose.

If only I could get my idiotic heart to believe it.

"You nervous?" asked Jason as I rejoined my bros.

"Yeah." At least admitting to nerves was better than admitting I was waiting for a girl. How dumb would that be? "It feels weird to be here."

"Hey, man. You have every right to be on this field. You freaking own it. We own it."

I thumped my pads. "That's right."

Jason ran deep and caught the next pass. I followed, this time forcing myself to tune out the stands. Devan threw a laser, slamming my pads making a hollow sound like a golf ball hitting a tree. I wrapped my arms around the ball, clutching it tight to my chest. That's what I did. I caught the short, fast ones when the quarterback was under pressure.

Coach gave me a nod. "Better."

Then I saw her. My mouth dropped open and I think I may have drooled. Hell, it was as if I'd been bench-pressing four hundred pounds and the barbell suddenly turned into a feather. Yeah, she wasn't just hot. She was amazing.

An unbelievable dime.

Standing out like a starlet, the sun made Vi's hair glimmer like burnished mahogany as the wind picked up the ends and swept the mane behind her like a waving flag.

When Lisa pointed to me, my tutor jumped up and down, waving both hands.

I think she liked me.

Grinning, I gave a quick thumbs-up.

"Williams?" Coach sounded pissed.

Shit.

"Yes, sir?"

"You ready to join the practice?"

"Born ready."

"It doesn't look like it to me."

"Throw me another slant," I said, taking off at an angle.

The ball came in like a bullet, aimed at my feet. Diving, I got my hands under it before the pigskin hit the ground.

"That's what I'm talkin' about," hollered Jason, clapping his hands.

Coach beckoned me over with a wave of his hand. "Do I need to worry about you, son?"

"No, sir."

"If I see you look at the stands one more time, I'm benching you, ya got it?"

"Yes, sir. Sorry, sir."

"I don't need to tell you that Michigan is one of the toughest opponents we'll face this year. We need this win and *you* need to keep your head in the game."

"You can count on me, sir."

He didn't need to tell me twice. I had my goals. I slammed the butt of my hand into the side of my helmet. Football and grades, man. That's my jam.

No women, right? What the hell had I been thinking?

Chapter Twelve

Vivian

My heart flew to my throat as the quarterback threw the ball into a pack of Michigan players mauling Cade. Then my jaw hit my chest. I had no idea what happened. Maybe I blinked, but somehow the dude managed to jump higher than everyone else, pluck the ball out of the air with one hand and pull it into his body while being tackled by five guys.

"Yes!" I shouted with the deafening cheers in the stands as the announcer bellowed, "Touchdown Gyrfalcons!"

Howling like a hyena, Lisa gave me a high-five. "That was amazing!"

"How in God's name did he catch that ball?"

She peered through her compact binoculars, pointing them at the student section. "A lifetime of practice, I'll wager."

"You found your grad student yet?"

"His name is Bryce, and...wait a minute...ooo." She gave me a nudge. "Found him."

"Cool."

"*Way* cool, 'cause he's with a bunch of dudes. Not a single female within talking distance."

"So...has he asked you out yet?"

"Nope."

"Surprising."

"I'm taking this one slow."

"Okaaay," I said as the Gyrfalcons kicked through the uprights, making the extra point. I smiled to myself for knowing that yet, by the cheers, everyone in the stands obviously already did. "Why slow?"

"I don't know. Keeping my options open, I guess."

"That can only mean one thing."

"What?"

"There's more than one grad of interest." I reached for the binoculars. "Where is he?"

"By the student section entrance, on the left, four rows up."

Good Lord, the guy looked like something out of *Law and Order*. Tall, dark hair, parted on the side, dark sunglasses. "Fits the bill."

Lisa took her binos. "Nice, huh?"

I reverted my attention to the field. "Hey, the other team's kicking again."

"They're punting. That's because they got a three and out."

"What?"

"They didn't make a first down, silly. Now they have to punt."

My heart did a fluttery thing—sort of happy, but nervous. That meant Cade would be back out there, which was exciting and terrifying at the same time.

I kept watching him, number forty-four, willing him to look my way. I didn't want him to look at me while he was trying to catch the ball, but he could give me a little wave as he ran off the field or something. Even when he wasn't in the game he stood on the sidelines with his back to the stands.

Of course it was awesome to watch him play. I could hardly believe the guys I'd met at the party were out there—Jason, Devan, and the others. I'd never realized how exciting football could be.

And nail-biting.

But by the end of the fourth quarter I had no reason to worry. We won by fourteen points. The band was still playing. Students were filing onto the field and Cade was out there shaking hands with all the Michigan guys who had looked as if they were going to kill him during the game.

Cripes, I felt wrung out like I'd been to two High Fitness classes back to back. "Well, that was nowhere near as bad as I thought it would be."

"Yeah," Lisa agreed, peering through her binoculars again. "These are awesome seats."

I checked for Cade again, but he'd been mobbed. Behind us, the stands were clearing out. "Where's your grad?"

"Lost him."

"Feel like a beer?" I asked. Why not? It was Saturday.

"Sounds good," Lisa said, tucking her binoculars into her hoodie pocket and leading the way along the row of seats.

"Vivian!" a dude called from the field. And I instantly knew who it was.

A zing lit up in my heart as I turned. Cade jogged right up to the wall with a smile so wide it nearly split his face in half. Wow, it was good to see him happy.

I leaned over the rail. "Hey! You were awesome out there."

"Thanks."

"That's my man." Jason came up behind, clapping him on the back. "His TD in the fourth quarter sealed the deal."

Cade gave him a fist bump. "Not to be outshined by your endzone laser grab in the first."

Lisa twisted around me. "If you keep playing like that, we'll be headed for the Rose Bowl for sure."

I stood there nodding in agreement like an idiot. I was so out of my element. Even with Lisa's tips. Though I'd also checked a few websites in a paltry attempt to learn how the game was played, football was still way foreign to me.

"Sooooo, ladies," said Jason. "We're celebrating our win. Want to join us?"

Cade's grin suddenly turned into a grimace. And he was looking straight at me. Couldn't his friend get a clue? The dude needed his space.

I shook my head. "I don't think—"

"Hell, yeah. We'll go." Lisa pulled out her phone. "Here?"

Jason threw his thumb over his shoulder. "Devan's."

I leaned farther over the rail directly above Cade. "Will you be there?"

Jason slapped his back. "Absolutely. Hell, his apartment is right next to our QB's, might as well knock a hole in the wall."

Cade crooked his finger, beckoning me to lean closer. "Since my arm has been twisted, it would be nice if you'd come. That is if you're okay with it, teach."

I swear about fifty cameras suddenly surrounded us.

Lisa practically knocked me over as if she were trying to get into a shot. "She's definitely okay."

"An hour," said Jason. "See you there."

Cade grabbed my hand and squeezed just as a reporter and cameraman tapped him on the shoulder.

Tugging me up, Lisa gave me a knowing eye. "He likes you. No matter what you say."

"No," I insisted. "He needs chick repellant. Again."

"My ass."

"Shut up."

Ignoring me, Lisa pulled me out of the stadium so fast, it was as if the place was on fire. "Why are you walking like a bat out of hell?"

"We need to change. Makeup. Hair. Clothes."

"It's just a stupid party."

She made a beeline toward the dorm. "Yeah? I just texted Bryce and he's dying to go with us."

"Who?"

"Sexy grad man."

"Right." I stopped. "Wait, you have his number?"

"Duh."

I should have figured. We practically ran across campus and as soon as we got to the room I texted Cade.

You OK with the party?

He fired right back: *Counting on you to be there, Teach.*

All right. But just for a little while. Lisa is bringing a friend. That OK?

Why not? It'll be a zoo.

Ugh.

Chapter Thirteen

Cade

I opened the door to my apartment just as Vi and her roommate stepped out of the elevator with a dude wearing a Gyrfalcon t-shirt who looked as if he'd already had a few too many beers.

Vi's gaze met mine and her face instantly brightened, making the stomach gyrations I had when a Michigan linebacker flipped me backward seem like calm seas. That move was awesome, though. I'd landed on my feet and dragged the bastard another five yards.

Vi looked beyond my shoulder. "Is the party in there?"

"Nah." I closed the door so she wouldn't see the mess. "That's my cave."

"You didn't tell me you lived next to Devan."

I don't know why I didn't tell her. I guess it wasn't relevant. "Yeah, but I did say I lived in the building."

She introduced Lisa's date, Bryce, a grad student in the law school. He looked like an apt apprentice for my attorney, except he still had the remnants of a California suntan.

"You grow up in Malibu?" I asked.

"How'd you guess?" Bryce flashed a cheesy grin and thrust out his palm. "Allow me to shake your hand, dude."

I took it. "You enjoy the game?"

"Hell yeah, but I'm talking about your defense. It was damned brilliant. Flawless," he said, slapping me on the back.

My hackles stood on end as we shouldered our way through a tunnel of people, the music from Devan's apartment had the bass turned up so loud the entire floor shook. "You want a beer?" I hollered over the din, making a path toward the kitchen while Vi and her friends managed to stay in my wake.

"Sounds good," said Bryce. "One for each of the ladies as well."

Devan had a keg sitting on the counter. I poured, then passed out the cups while Bryce sidled up to me like he was my best bro. "So, how'd you cope while you were waiting for your trial?"

I shrugged, giving him one of the dead-eyed glares meant to put the fear of God in the hearts of linebackers before the ball is snapped. "Tried to stay busy. Worked. Took some online classes."

"I'll bet it drove you insane."

It majorly fucked with my mind, but I was doing my best not to think about it. I didn't reply and slung my arm around Vi's shoulder while I took a long pull on my beer.

"Hey." Bryce nudged me, leaning in so close I got an unpleasant whiff of sour breath. "What would you have done if the verdict hadn't gone your way?"

"Ah..." I gulped, feeling like a rat was crawling up my back. Would this guy drop it already? "I guess I wouldn't have had a choice. Convicts rarely do."

Bryce smirked. "How much did your attorney ding you for?"

"Too much." I ground my teeth, willing myself to take charge of the intense desire to bury my fist in Mr. Inquisitorial's snout. I scanned the crammed apartment and spotted his date dancing with Jason. "Hey, I just want to put it behind me, okay? Why don't you find Lisa and see if she wants another beer?"

"Yeah. Sorry." Bryce thumped his forehead with the heel of his hand. "You just won the first game of the year and I'm running my mouth about your trial."

"Unbelievable," Vi mumbled behind her cup as the grad student moved into the swarming hive.

I took a long drink. "It's not the first time. Won't be the last."

Someone shoved her into me making my beer slosh across my shirt. She tensed, cringing. "Oh man, I'm so sorry."

"Not your fault. This place is so crowded I think we're all holding each other up." I grabbed a napkin off the counter and wiped my shirt.

She set her cup down and looked longingly at the door. "I need some air."

"Want to go for a walk?" God, I was lame. Aside from my grandma, I don't think I've ever asked anyone to go for a walk.

"I'm dying to get out of here, but what about you?" She gave my arm an affectionate nudge. "Don't you want to celebrate with your teammates?"

Scratching beneath my cap, I surveyed the room. Bryce and Lisa were out of sight. Jason was dancing with about five girls. Devan was by the fridge retelling a play-by-play account of the game, and the others were all intermixed among half-drunk students. "I don't think anyone would notice if we slipped away."

"Let me tell Lisa we're going." Vi started for the living room but got nowhere. "Never mind. I'll send her a text."

I managed to pull her to the door only because I'm bigger and stronger than most people. But the hallway wasn't any better. "Hold onto my waist and stay behind me, I'll be your blocker."

Vi's giggle was infectious, making me grin. Her fingertips tingled through the thin fabric of my t-shirt. On the way past, I glanced at the door to my apartment and nearly stopped. Lord knew I wanted to. But the needling guilt at the back of my mind convinced me to keep going.

Some dude gave me a high-five. "Good game!"

"Thanks," I said, making a beeline to the open elevator which was occupied by a couple necking. I mean the only reason they weren't making babies was because they still had their clothes on.

Vi cleared her throat and turned away. The problem was we were surrounded by mirrors.

I swiped a hand across my eyes and whispered, "Awkward."

She just snorted but once we stepped outside she burst out laughing. "I should have told them to get a room."

"I don't think they would have heard you."

"Are you tired?" Vi asked as she led the way toward the shore of Lake Mendota.

The truth? I'd been tired for months. I hadn't slept. I felt like a zombie on caffeine. "I'm too wound up to be tired."

"I still can't believe you caught that pass. Cripes, so many Michigan players tackled you, and yet you still managed to hold onto the ball."

"It's what I was born to do. I love being out there."

"By the way you play, it sure shows." Vi ran her finger along a line of mortar in the brick wall edging the sidewalk. "But how do you deal with all the attention? I mean, it's not just the media. Guys like Bryce must get in your face all the time."

"They do." A new tic beside my eye twitched. "I'd be lying if I said it doesn't get to me sometimes. But we're coached on how to speak to the media. What to say. How to say it."

"That's good. Interesting. What are the most important things to remember?"

"When talking to the media?" I asked.

"Mm hmm."

"Always compliment the other team. Give credit to your teammates. Never sound too arrogant. Be polite. That sort of thing."

"I guess that keeps you from getting into trouble."

"I wish it did," I mumbled, my gaze dropping to my toes.

My gut suddenly felt like the bricks from the wall had piled up in my colon. I'd thought about it nearly every waking hour since my arrest. I wasn't a bad dude. I was like every other college kid out there who played ball. Sure, we got hyped up, but that was part of the game.

Stopping outside the boathouse, Vi took my hands, then dropped them as if they were on fire and backed a step. "Sorry. I know it can't be easy for you." She threw her arms out with a nervous laugh. "That's why you're here with someone like me, right?"

"Huh?" What did she mean, someone like her? If I could have a girl like her, I'd be the luckiest man in the world—if my head weren't so fucked up. I licked my lips about to ask what she was talking about, but she held up her hand, commanding me to keep my mouth shut.

"What I want to ask is, are you doing okay?" Her warm palm covered my heart, making my breath catch. "In here."

I stared at her with the intensity of a tortured soul. If only I could tell her about the rage that's always simmering beneath the surface. But I'm not a bleeding heart. And talking about it would only make the fire inside me turn into an inferno.

"I'm fine," I mumbled, shrugging.

Those intoxicating fingers slid away far too soon. "Maybe to everyone else you're fine. I know I haven't been around you that long, but I sense your tension like you're a rubber band about to snap."

Figure that. I knew this woman for all of two weeks and she was the only person in my life who was able to read me like a book. My jaw twitched—I swear that one was becoming a permanent tic. If only I could spill all the anger pent up inside, but I wasn't about to do that, not to her, not now. Maybe not this year. "Things will get better."

"Do you ever see her?"

Every muscle in my body clenched. I knew what she meant and she was getting too close to the trigger. One more inch and I might explode. "No," I said in a deep, seething voice I hardly recognized.

"Is she still a student?"

"Graduated."

"But why did she accuse you?"

God, Vi just needed to let it go. I squeezed my fists so tight, my fingernails dug into my palms...and I'd trimmed them this morning. "Aside from being a psychopath?"

"It sounds insane." The breeze picked up Vi's hair and she tucked it behind her hear.. "Is she still in Madison?"

"I don't know and I don't care." I tugged her along the lakeshore path. "Can we talk about something else?"

"Yes." She stopped me again. "It's important for me to say that...well, I'm glad you were assigned to be my student. You're an okay dude."

"Just okay?"

"Hey, I'm your tutor."

Right now, I wished she were anything but. Then again, it was best that she was off-limits. Even though she looked like sin in jeans that fit like they were painted on. And at five-feet-ten and all legs, there was a whole lot of paint. Everything about her turned me on. Full lips that closed in a pout, begging to be kissed. Intelligent eyes missing nothing, assessing everything. And the breeze picked up her wild mane of chestnut hair, making her look like a model in a commercial for a mega-force blow drier.

I shouldn't be here.

"Hey." Vi took my hand. "Why do I sense you're a million miles away?"

Because if I didn't distance myself, I'd do something I'd regret. But I couldn't tell her what I really felt, so I just raised my shoulder to my ear. "I have no idea what you're talking about."

"I'm sorry I brought it up..." Her gaze drifted aside.

"I guess you're curious just like everyone else."

"Maybe, but I ought to respect your need to put it all behind you. I'm sure my blurting out questions doesn't help."

I wanted to forget. But I hadn't been able to put the whole mess out of my mind...unless I was on the field. Or with Vi when she wasn't asking questions.

"So, do you do any community service?" she asked, sounding as if she was trying to pep me up. "I see Madison players on the news sometimes."

"We all do. Hospitals, food banks, that sort of thing."

"I think that's awesome. So many kids idolize you."

I wasn't so sure about that now. I guess I'd find out next time we visited the children's ward at the hospital.

As we rounded the bend near the park, she broke into a run and headed for a tree. "Look," she said, picking up a foam football. She tossed it up and caught it. "So, I've been teaching you accounting. Why don't you show me a few moves?"

One corner of my mouth dumbly ticked up. "Okay."

I wanted to show her some moves all right, just not the kind she had in mind.

Yes, I was a complete and utter idiot. A total masochist. But Vi was turning into a drug and I needed more.

I trotted toward the middle of the field while the woman raced ahead. Obviously, she hadn't been tackled thirty-or-so times today.

"Is this right?" she asked, bending over like a center about to the hike the ball.

I nearly choked. With a sexy, heart-shaped ass like Vivian Ellis' there wouldn't be a player on the field paying an iota of attention to the game.

My hands itched to slide tight against her crotch urge her to snap the ball. Except I'd drop it. Instead, I moved into a shotgun position. "When I say three-nineteen, hike the ball and run wide."

Vi's ass waggled as she looked over her shoulder. "Run where?"

"Just run down the field and I'll throw it to you."

"Got it." The damned ass wiggled again. "I'm ready."

God knew I was ready. "Three-nineteen," I bellowed, deciding not to draw out my torture.

She hiked the ball as if she'd been playing center for decades, though she ran straight down the field on her toes like freaking ballerina. I threw the ball nice and easy but she just kind of batted the thing away like it was a fly.

"Why didn't you catch it?" I spread my hands to my sides. "That was an easy one."

"Maybe for you."

I realized she wasn't wearing her glasses. "Can't you see it?"

She picked up the ball. "I'm wearing contacts. I'm just not used to running and catching. I'm more of a yoga, dance fitness kind of girl."

"Didn't your dad play catch with you?"

"No dad." She tossed the ball at me. "At least not one who hung around."

My heart twisted like I'd just come upon an abused kid or something. Vi never told me about her father. Come to think of it, we'd spent so much time talking about me, she hadn't told me much about herself. "Then we'd better start by throwing a few."

I figured the woman had to be a natural athlete because after a couple of drops she didn't miss a single pass. I may have been going easy on her, but I still reckoned she'd give Wonder Woman a run for her money.

"You want to try again?" she asked, pointing to the ground as if she was planning to hike.

I wasn't about to stare at her ass one more time without doing something stupid, so I took the ball and crouched into the center position. "I'll go out. You play quarterback."

Everything went well—I hiked, ran, she threw, I caught it. Except she ran for me, roaring like a Viking on attack. Laughing, I tucked the ball high and tight and started shuffling backward, but she didn't stop. Taking a flying leap, she wrapped her arms around my waist. Ready for impact, I planted my feet wide, but Vi hit me just right.

Together we toppled backward toward the turf as she nailed me.

"Ow," she half-sang, half-laughed.

My belly shook as I laughed with her. No joke, she'd make a damned good corner. "You okay?" I asked, her body sprawled on top of me, covering me with those curves. Man, she turned me on like no one I'd ever met before. Soft, perfect breasts molded into my chest while she stared into my eyes like a woman who needed to be kissed.

A pink tongue slipped to the corner of her mouth. "Uh huh."

My hands grew a mind of their own and slid around her waist. I raised my chin, willing her to close the distance. Lowering her lashes, a quick gasp caught in her throat as her lips caressed mine.

With my next heartbeat, I slid my hand behind her neck, our lips fusing like two lovers who'd been separated for far too long. As our tongues entwined, flares of primitive desire shot through me. For the love of God, I'd been living like a monk for over a year. And ever since this woman walked into my life, I've thought of little else.

Whenever I closed my eyes I saw Vi.

Yes, I admit that each morning when the alarm sounded, I pictured her in the top she didn't end up wearing to my party, or in sweats, or the first time I saw her in the shadows of the library entrance. It didn't matter. I saw her and my need for her grew every single day. And now I craved her like a starved castaway who'd been stranded alone on an island for years.

Vi moved her hips, rubbing my erection, sending my mind into a frenzy. My need ratcheted to new heights. I was harder than steel. I slid my fingers into her hair—that glorious mane of silk I'd been dying to touch. As I moved against her, she moaned into my mouth.

I was on fire.

In public.

And I totally needed to stop.

Damn.

Panting, she took her weight on the palms of her hands. As soon as her gaze met mine, her breath caught and her eyebrows slanted inward as if she were horrified.

"Oh, God, I'm sorry," she said, rolling off me.

I reached out, grabbing her hand. I wanted, needed, craved to pull her back over me.

But I didn't.

"No apologies," I growled, trying to catch my breath.

She tugged her fingers away and sat up.

So did I.

"You don't need another silly woman lusting after you." Planting her face in her palms, she shook her head. "I shouldn't have tackled you."

"I shouldn't have kissed you."

"No."

"But I liked it."

"You did?" Her head snapped up, her lips swollen and red from kissing. "I don't understand. Back in the library I tried to give you a hug—not to kiss you, but because you were hurting, and you went stiff as a board."

I glanced away. I probably should have done the same this time. Except her irresistible body had been on top of me. "Look," I started, but damned if I could pull the words together. "Um...I told you about my goals, right?"

"Uh huh." She held up two fingers. "Win a championship and improve your GPA."

"And there's a third."

"What is it?"

I grabbed a handful of grass and yanked it out by the roots. "No women."

"Oh." Hell, the disappointment in her voice was palpable.

But now I'd said it, I had to stick to my guns. No matter how much I wanted to wrap her in my arms and kiss her until the sun went down. No matter how much I was going to relive this moment after my alarm went off every morning.

Before I could think of some way to explain, she grabbed the ball and stood. "All right. Let's pretend the kiss never happened, okay?"

"Good idea."

Yeah, right. This moment would insure I didn't sleep. For the rest of the year I'll be lying in bed awake with a hard-on while my entire body aches to hold her in my arms.

I almost pulled her back down. But then bile churned in my gut. I couldn't risk taking a chance with a woman. Not even a gift as precious as Vivian. No way in hell could I survive anything close to what I went through last year.

The trial nearly killed me. Killed my chances at a future. Killed the dreams my dad had for me.

"Throw me a bomb." I forced myself to my feet and started to run out for a pass but as I turned, she wasn't there. "Vi?"

"See you Monday," she called from the sidewalk.

Damn, she didn't even turn around.

Chapter Fourteen

Vivian

Why did I do it? Why did I tackle him? Why did I set myself up in the first place by going to the party? I knew it would be insane. Why did I even go to the game? I'm not Cade's bodyguard. Heck, the dude is a behemoth. He can fend off anyone he wants. I wouldn't be surprised if ten guys attacked him in an alley, he'd walk away leaving all of them bloodied in his wake.

I still can't believe I saw him run at least ten yards with five enormous football players hanging off him.

Cripes, I'm an imbecile.

I pushed into the dorm room and made a beeline for my bed. Flopping onto my back, I squeezed the foam football against my chest and let out a wretched groan.

"You all right?"

My eyes snapped open. "Lisa?" She was on her bed, hugging my Aquaman pillow. "What are you doing here?"

"Uh...last I checked, I was living here."

"Yeah, but you were out with Bryce."

"No. Bryce was out with himself."

"Huh?" I asked, swinging my legs over the side of the bed.

"Let's just say he had a bit too much to drink and decided Devan Thomas was a far more interesting conversationalist."

"Turd."

"Mega turd." Lisa curled up on her side. "But what about you? Why the woeful groan?"

"Don't ask."

"No, no. You don't come in here, flop on the bed like the world's ending and zip your lips. Out with it, girl."

The pillow sailed across the room and landed on my face. Seriously, I needed to chain the thing to my headboard.

I tossed Aquaman aside. "I texted you."

"Yeah, you said you were getting some air." She scooted up and tucked her legs beneath her. "What? Did you go to Cade's apartment? How did you end up with an effing football?"

"Don't jump to conclusions," I sniped, giving her a ginormous eye roll. "We went for a walk along Lake Mendota. I found the ball under a tree, we played some, and when it was my turn to play quarterback I tackled him."

Her eyes bugged in disbelief. "You? Tackled a six-three two hundred fifty-pound dude?"

I chewed my bottom lip. "I kinda think he let me knock him down."

I rolled over and faced the wall while Lisa walked across the room and stood beside my bed. My elbow hurt. My knee was scraped. How did those guys survive an entire hour of pummeling every weekend?

She picked up the ball. "So, you tackled a guy who probably got tackled twenty times today. What, did you break his arm?"

"No, thank God. The entire team would never forgive me."

"Well, then, you'd better tell me the rest."

I groaned again and shifted up, resting my back against the headboard. "I have no idea how it happened. One second we were laughing and the next I had my tongue down his throat..." I hesitated while the kiss played out in my mind, wishing it weren't so darned *memorable*. "...or was it he had his tongue down mine?"

The football dropped with a thud. "Holy shit."

Pretending like kissing Cade was no big deal, I checked my elbow. It wasn't bleeding, but a big bruise had started spreading down my arm. "It gets worse."

"You had sex in public?"

"God, no!" Though that might have been better than... "After we came up for air he told me he'd sworn off women."

"The dick! What a freaking asshole." Lisa kicked the ball, sending it skidding like a whirly bird under her bed. "He kisses you and then tells you to take a hike?"

"Yeah."

My freaking mind must still be numb from practically keeling over. He kissed me like there was no tomorrow. He kissed me as if I were the only woman left on the planet. Like he'd die if he didn't. He clung to me as if he were afraid I might pull away. His hips rocked against...oh my God, did they rock.

Did I miss something?

Yeah. The part where he doesn't want a woman. Duh! The guy just spent a year proving his innocence to the world because of one messed-up female.

No wonder he had his goals written inside his notebook. But if I were him, I'd put the third anti-woman clause in bold letters and show it to all unsuspecting tutors.

"Well, at least you learned he's an asshole now before he steals your heart."

Except he already has.

My gaze flicked to Lisa's for a heartbeat. "Right, the stupid kiss is nothing I can't put behind me."

"You going to be okay?"

"Of course."

"You don't look like it."

I patted my pockets to make sure I still had my phone. "Come on, let's go get pizza and talk about anything other than guys and football."

"What about movie stars?"

"Sure. As long as they're green and live on Mars."

Chapter Fifteen

Cade

The next month passed in a blur. To be honest, between my heavy load of classes, practices, and away games, I didn't have much time to do anything else but sleep and eat.

At least that's what I told myself no matter how much Vi consumed my every-other thought.

Our tutoring sessions were killing me, yet despite my love for the game, studying with Vivian Ellis was the thing I looked forward to most.

And somehow I managed to learn while sitting next to the only woman on campus who had my number. I mean it killed me just to breathe whenever I sat beside her. Vi used the most intoxicating shampoo. It smelled like coconuts and mangoes and sunshine. My heart stopped every time the woman smiled. Like a lovesick teen, I sometimes put my hand on the desk beside hers, whishing our pinky fingers would touch.

But they never did.

Ever since I kissed her, she's been all about accounting. Even when I ask her a personal question, she gives me a brief answer and refocuses her attention on the lesson.

She has never been rude. Never brusque. But always somewhat distant and exceptionally controlled.

God, I admired her for that.

And I'd basically asked her for it.

Worse, I'd kicked myself every day since.

"Are you taking a break or do you need me to pull the bar off your chest?"

I opened my eyes to find Jason bending over me in the weight room, his hands ready to take the weights.

How many reps had I done? Jeez, I needed to stop daydreaming.

I pushed up the bar and settled it back in the cradle. "Sorry. Must have lost my concentration."

"You getting enough sleep?"

I sat up and wiped my face with a towel. "Hell, no. Is anyone?"

"I think Devan sleeps like death."

"How would you know?"

"He never answers his phone even though he says he keeps it next to his bed."

"Why are you calling him in the middle of the night?"

Jason's nostrils flared with his smirk. "Good thing you're built like a tank."

"Isn't it, stork?"

"Just remember, I can run a hell of a lot faster than you."

"Maybe, but never forget you're more breakable."

"That's why they bother putting your ass on the field, dude. Sometimes it takes a tank."

I laughed and flicked his bare thigh with my towel. Wide receivers. All of them had egos the size of the stadium. What they didn't understand was guys like me who were able to block two hundred fifty pound linebackers made it possible for them to make plays.

As we headed for the locker room, my body felt like it had been steamrollered. Not because today's practice had been grueling, but because I'd taken some pretty brutal hits in Saturday's game. Thank God it was Monday. That gave me five days to recover for homecoming.

And we had to win. We were playing Minnesota. Losing to them was like losing to your grandma...when she was swinging a baseball bat, of course.

I took a quick shower, donned my hoodie, and headed for the nearest food joint. A blast of icy air shot through me as I walked outside. A good old Wisconsin winter was coming. Of that there could be no doubt. Days were getting shorter and there'd be snow before Thanksgiving. There always was. This was my fourth year in the northern Midwest and I had no illusions.

As I trotted past the student's gym, a familiar scent made me stop. Made my heart leap in ten different directions.

Vivian.

She plowed into my chest and jolted, skittering. "Gah. Sorry!"

I grabbed her shoulders. "Hey. What are you doing here?"

Shifting her gaze to my face, she let out a sharp gasp. "Cade?" She tightened her grip on the strap of her yoga mat as she blushed. Even her forehead turned red. "Um...I'm going to a fitness class. You?"

"Just finished practice. Thought I'd grab something to eat before we hit the books. You want to join me?"

"I'd better not, else I'll be eating salad for a month."

"For missing one lousy yoga class?"

"It's a chisel class, really. Weights, stretching, cardio."

"That sounds like something I could get into."

The corner of her mouth turned up as she threw her thumb over her shoulder. "Why don't you come along?"

I peered through the glass doors and a ghost walked past. My knees went weak. A sweat broke out on my forehead. "What the...?"

"Are you okay? You just lost all the color in your face."

I swiped a hand across my eyes while ice pulsed through my blood. I swear the shadow was the person who sat behind me in court. The one who whispered taunts.

Vi tugged on my sleeve. "Hey, dude, I asked if you're all right."

"Yeah. Sorry. I'm starved."

She looked toward the door. "You sure—"

"I'm fine." I flicked her mat. "I'll see you tonight?"

"Of course." Starting away, she glanced over her shoulder. "How was your Accounting midterm? You get your grade yet?"

I grinned. "Aced it."

Clapping, she gave a little hop. I don't care how cool she played it. She still liked me. "I knew you would. Congrats!"

"Couldn't have done it without you, teach."

"Thanks."

"Are you going to be at the homecoming game?" I asked, while something kick-started in my belly that I fought to ignore. Sure, I liked her, too, but I needed to keep it chill.

No. More. Kissing. No matter how much I wanted to pull her into my arms and replay the dynamite kiss in the park...without the ending, of course.

She gave me a sassy wink. At least I thought it was a wink. Or was it the light reflecting on her glasses? "Are you planning to win?"

She winked. I know she did.

Not to be outdone, I waggled my eyebrows. "Bet your ass."

"Well then, go Gyrfalcons!"

"You better watch yourself, you're starting to sound like a fan." My tongue slipped to the corner of my mouth. "So, you'll be there?"

"I'm thinking about it." She flicked her head, tossing her ponytail off her shoulder. "Why not? Maybe if I watched football I'd find a boyfriend who might stick around."

My jaw dropped while she danced into the gym. Not only had she rendered me speechless, my gut twisted, my jaw twitched, and I was suddenly ready to bury my fist in any dude's face if he so much as checked out Vi's ass.

"*What freaking boyfriend?*" I wanted to shout. How in God's name could she say something like that and just walk away, giving me an eyeful of her yoga-pant-clad ass. An ass I'd been dying to sink my fingers into ever since our first tutoring session. If only she knew how much she tortured me. A good kind of torture but sticking to my guns and being a monk was harder than I ever dreamed.

I clenched my fist around the strap of my gym bag. Why did Vi need a boyfriend? If anyone hurt her, I'd kill him—or convince the bastard to go out for football so I could severely injure him without being arrested.

Chapter Sixteen

Vivian

After my fitness class, a pair of pink cross trainers came into my line of sight as I slid my mat into its harness.

"Hey, aren't you Cade William's new girlfriend?"

What. The. Hell?

I swear, all the blood in my body rushed to my face. I'd fielded a few comments after the incident in the library. And the Michigan game had been a month ago. The Gyrfalcon news had published a picture of Cade reaching up and squeezing my hand, but my face had been partially shaded by my hat and, aside from Lisa, no one had figured out it was me.

I straightened and swung my mat over my shoulder. "What gives you that idea?"

I'd seen this girl in the gym a few times and she reminded me of one of those narcissistic models on *Project Runway*. Everything about her was perfect, from her skin to her blonde hair to the way she carried herself—and her face. In fact, I wondered if it would crack if she smiled.

She held out her phone. "You're on the Gyrfalcon Feathers blog site."

I'd never heard of it. But sure enough, there was a picture of me on top of Cade in the park…kissing.

What the heck? That was a month ago!

Shrinking, I checked for the nearest escape, but there wasn't one close enough

How had that picture ended up on some blog, and who the hell had taken it? Jeez, I hoped Cade hadn't seen it. I didn't remember anyone following us, not that I'd been paying much attention.

I did my best to look unruffled, as if I weren't about to die of embarrassment. "Old news. We're not dating," I said, trying to keep it as simple as possible. Anyway, Cade's and my love life was none of her business.

Even if we had a love life.

"That's good."

Why?

I suddenly wanted to slap her. "Who runs the blog?" I asked instead.

"I have no idea." She pocketed her phone and held out her hand. "I'm Lexi."

I shook it. Her fingers were icy. "Vi."

She smiled—sort of. "You looked awesome in class. Have you been training for a long time?"

I took a sidestep away, wanting to avoid her like the plague. "Ever since I started going to Madison."

Of course she followed me. "Good for you. I just started."

I slung my mat over my shoulder. "You a freshman?"

"No—a junior. I transferred from the Milwaukee campus at the beginning of the year."

"What's your major?"

"Pre-law."

"Cool." I decided not to mention that I roomed with a pre-law major. "Well, see you around," I said as I took off for the locker room to put on a pair of jeans before my tutoring session.

Though I ran to the School of Business, when I pushed into the study room Cade was already waiting for me. He sat behind the desk with his laptop open. It made him look huge, wide shoulders bent over, his enormous fingers poised on the keyboard.

God, the man *was* massive.

When he looked up, my traitorous stomach flipped. My breath caught and my palms perspired. I should be accustomed to seeing him by now, but every time those light blue eyes focused on me I went weak at the knees.

And there seemed to be nothing I could do about it.

My gaze slid to the clock as I tucked a lock of hair that had escaped my ponytail behind my ear. "You're early."

He usually came in a couple of minutes late. "Thought I'd surprise you."

"How was dinner?" I asked, slinging my backpack onto the desk and trying not to notice the way he scraped his teeth over his bottom lip. And definitely ignoring the zinging butterflies in my stomach.

Cade dragged my chair up beside him. "It filled the void. Conversation was lacking, though."

I sat. "Don't tell me you ate alone."

"Okay."

Whoa, he did eat alone. I wonder where his groupies were.

I opened my laptop and checked the syllabus. "Looks like you're starting cost accounting next week. Cool—something new to tackle."

"Tackling's my jam." He leaned in and peered at my screen. "Tell me, what rocks about Cost Accounting?"

Once we settled in I usually was able to check my emotions and focus on the lesson. But today he put his elbow on the desk, propped his head in his hand and intently stared at me while I gave an example of assigning costs a company might incur when printing a t-shirt—exactly how it was laid out in the book.

He stared.

I turned the screen toward him. "See?"

He stared.

I finally sucked in a deep breath and met his gaze. God, if eyes could sizzle, he'd mastered the art. I think I stopped breathing.

The corner of his mouth ticked up.

"Are you paying attention?" I asked, putting on my best boss-lady voice as if I weren't wondering how sturdy the desk was...or if I ought to lock the door. Yes, he was turning me into a total sex maniac. "Or do you have attention deficit today?"

The man slid his little pinky over mine.

Good Lord, I gasped so loudly, a person might have thought he'd slid his tongue into my mouth. Which I definitely would never allow him to do again.

It took every ounce of willpower in my soul, but I pulled my hand away and crossed my arms. "Must be the latter." After all, he's the one who said he'd sworn off women. And I couldn't blame him.

At least for now.

And I wasn't going to be his downfall. Not when the Gyrfalcons had a chance at a top-notch bowl game. Yeah, I knew that, too.

But I'll be darned if I didn't want to confront him...to tell him not all women are out to ruin his life.

I scooted my chair away from him a few inches. "So, what's next for you? Rumors are you're planning to enter the NFL draft." At least that's what Lisa told me. I think we were both turning into football maniacs. I even purchased tickets to the homecoming game—in the el-cheapo student section, of course.

He rubbed the back of his neck. "I'm hoping to but that's a secret."

"If you go pro, what will happen to your education?"

"Well, now you know why I'm taking extra classes. And if I don't have enough credits by the end of this year I'll study in the off-season until I do."

"But why not wait?"

"I'm only a junior because I missed last year. You're graduating, aren't you?"

"Yes."

"Well then, you won't miss me if I'm not here."

"That's not the point." His goals were the point. But why was I making his goals my problem? "Isn't it true if you enter the draft you'll be making so much money you won't need a degree?"

"Doesn't matter. I want my degree and I want football."

"Because of your dad?"

"Damn right." Cade rapped the desk with his knuckles. "Besides, anything can happen. Players get hurt and any way you look at it, their careers are short. The average pro only lasts three to four years."

"That's all?"

"Some last sixteen or more, but not usually tight ends like me because we get pretty banged up. The body can only take so much punishment."

There were so many details about the game that I'd never considered, and my head spun with a hundred questions. "But Jason's a senior and he's coming back next year."

"He's a red shirt."

I think I understood but I still arched my eyebrows and rolled my hand through the air, asking for an explanation.

"That means he didn't play his freshman year. He's good enough to declare for the draft at the end of the year, but he'd probably be a fifth or sixth rounder—maybe have to be a free agent."

"Does that matter?"

"The dude's got talent, but he was a late bloomer. If he plays college ball next year, he could move up to first or second round."

"So...that's worthwhile? Didn't you say it's a risk?"

"Everything's a risk in this game, but if Jason wants to earn the big bucks he'll come back to Madison for another season."

"But not you?"

"I'm getting old."

I blew a raspberry. "What, you're twenty-one?"

"Twenty-two."

"That's not old."

Leaning closer, he brushed his knuckle across my cheek, sending shivers down my spine. "It is in this business."

I licked my lips, daring to meet his gaze. Strike me dead, but the man was sexy. "I...um...thought you'd sworn off women."

"I did."

"Why?" I whispered even though I knew the answer.

"Because a woman almost ruined my life."

"But all women aren't psychotic," I said, *finally*. I'd been waiting for the opportunity to say it for over a month.

"No?"

I crossed my arms and tilted my nose up. "I'm not."

He closed his laptop and kissed me on top of the head like I was five. "Look, I can't deal with anything else right now. And relationships mess with a man's head."

As Cade left the room he mumbled something that sounded like. "*No matter how much I want to.*"

But I wasn't sure.

When the door closed, I dropped my head back. This assignment was going to kill me. There was no doubt the chemistry between us was red hot. And he's the one who'd started it. Why did he have to touch my finger? I was totally in control before his little pinky slid over and embraced mine.

God, the intensity in that moment was almost as if he'd pulled me into his arms. Next, I'll be having an orgasm every time he looks into my eyes.

Who plays pinky fingers with their tutor?

Who does such a thing when they're not planning on going further?

Cripes, it's as if we're back in junior high.

I groaned. *Maybe I need to get laid.*

The problem?

The only person I'd remotely consider sleeping with just walked out the door.

Chapter Seventeen

Cade

Game Day

Sitting on the bench across from my locker, I pulled Dad's plain silver cross out from under my jersey and kissed it.

"This one's for you, Dad. It's all for you."

Jason slid beside me and I stuffed the cross back into place. "You ready?"

"Ready to eat me some Minnesota butt!"

He slapped me on the back. "That's what I like to hear."

I stood and pulled him up. "Question is, are you fast enough to beat out their five-star corner?"

"Faster."

I threw a fist into the air. "You going to leave him in the dust?"

"You kidding? I'll make him eat my dust." Jason picked up his helmet. "If he can manage to get close enough."

Devan strutted past us and grabbed our jerseys. "Are you ladies planning to stand around yapping all day or are you ready to play ball?" he shouted loud enough to make the lockers rattle.

The entire team roared as the three of us locked elbows and led the run out onto the field. I forced myself not to look into the stands.

The shouts from the crowd made the stadium shake, amping up my adrenalin. I knew Vi was in the student section and felt her eyes on me. And from the first snap of the ball, having her there infused me with power. I was faster, I hit harder.

But no matter how many touchdowns the Gyrfalcon offense scored, our defense made too many mistakes. At the end of the fourth quarter every man on the O-line was spent. I could have sworn I'd run at least a hundred routes, made a gazillion blocks, and had been tackled so many times my lungs were about to collapse. Twenty-two seconds remained on the clock and Coach had taken our final timeout.

From the sidelines, Devan ran back into the huddle.

I ground my back molars and eyed him. None of us wanted this blood-bath to go into overtime.

But we were only on the fifty yard-line—too far for a field goal. We had time to make one more play, get another twenty yards, and kick for the win.

The problem?

Our kicker was a freshman. And his accuracy was for shit. If we settled for a field goal, we'd probably end up going into overtime. And I'd never been this spent in my life. Yeah, I should be confident.

But I wasn't.

We needed a miracle.

I prayed our quarterback and Coach had come up with something badass enough to blow us all away.

Devan looked straight at me. "You up for a Red Eighty?"

My throat went dry. We hadn't used that play since my sophomore year. "Hell, yeah," I croaked. "You sure?"

He gave me a cocky smirk as if the entire game weren't riding on the next play. "Unless your arm has forgotten how to throw."

In truth, I could throw farther than anyone on the team. Licking my lips, I glanced at Jason. "You still outrunning that ornery dweeb?"

A bead of sweat dripped from the point of the wide receiver's nose. "One more time, man."

Devan slapped me on the back. "You got this."

I rubbed the cross under my jersey and looked to heaven.

You'd better be watching, Dad, 'cause I'm gonna to end the game right here.

We broke the huddle and lined up, except I didn't quite stack in my usual spot, but close enough to it not to alert Minnesota to a trick play. I eyed the linebacker across from me like I'd been doing all afternoon. He pursed his lips, throwing a taunting kiss.

I grinned and winked at the bastard.

Eat me.

Devan rattled off a number of bogus cadences, trying to pull them offsides but no one budged. Then a burst of lightning raced through my blood when he bellowed, "Red Eighty!"

As soon as the center hiked the ball, I blocked my man, changed my route, ran behind Devan, and caught his lateral. The Minnesota defense shifted directions, making a beeline for me. I took one look downfield.

Shit!

Jason's defender was all over his ass. The only way to ensure the ball didn't end up in the wrong hands was to overthrow by a hair. Worse, I had to put it on the money with no margin for error.

Was I that good? Devan was more accurate for sure.

You can do anything you set your mind to, son.

In a nanosecond, goosebumps covered my skin. I knew my heart was racing but it thundered in my ears in a slow and steady thrum.

Dad was watching. So was Vi. Mom, back in Jersey, too.

I breathed in as, out of the corner of my eye, the asshole linebacker dove for my feet. Slipping away, I danced two steps forward and let the ball fly on the run. As it left my fingers, an ape hit me from behind. My head whipped back as I slammed into the ground like I'd plummeted off the high dive and hit with a belly flop.

Pushing up on my side, dirt dangled from my facemask as I gaped downfield.

My. God.

Jason was doing the Shiggy in the endzone.

Swiping the dirt clod away, I rolled to my back just as a boat-shaped cloud sailed past.

Did you see that Dad?

Gasping for air, I pushed to my feet. I never should have doubted myself. I was back, and if that move didn't impress the NFL scouts, I didn't know what would. Hell, come morning I'd be black and blue, but right now, nothing was going to take away the power I felt. Flexing my fingers, I broke into a run.

"We did it!" I yelled, leaping through the air and smacking pads with my bro.

Only when we ran off the field did I look to the stands. I knew where she was, halfway up in the center of the student section. She stood out like a swan among geese, waving a pompom. I took off my hat and pumped it in the air while I pointed her way.

"You've got it bad dude," Jason said, running beside me.

Snorting, I jabbed my bro in the pads. "I have no idea what you're talking about."

"Your tutor. She has your number."

I shoved my helmet back on my head. "The only people who have my number are the scouts."

"Yeah, right."

Maybe I did like her more than I should. But our sessions would be coming to an end soon. I probably wouldn't see her much in the off season either.

But for now, I liked having her there.

In the stands.

Watching...*me*.

As we approached the sidelines, Coach pulled me into a bear hug. "Congratulations. You're the game's MVP. You ready to talk to the media?"

"Yes, sir."

I chuckled. There were five other guys on the team who ought to be MVP as well, but I guess they picked the dude who threw the winning pass for this one. As I stood in front of the cameras, I looked to the stands and my heart sank.

Vi was gone.

And I had no right to be so disappointed.

Chapter Eighteen

Cade

I checked my work with the answer key and tapped my pen on the paper. "I think I'm ready for tomorrow's exam."

Vi leaned in and drew a star. "Excellent."

My eyes rolled back with my inhale. Today she smelled like a tropical island—coconut, pineapple, a hint of mint. "Did you start using a new shampoo?" I asked, catching a lock of shiny chestnut hair and drawing it to my nose.

She flicked it over her shoulder and away from my fingers. "Cheap stuff. It was on sale at the drug store."

"Well, it smells good."

The door suddenly opened and Professor Lundgren popped his head in. Jeez, I nearly fell out of my chair. I mean, I'd been fiddling with my tutor's hair behind closed doors, thinking we had all the privacy in the world. Besides, the man had never interrupted one of our sessions before.

"Looks like you're the last ones here. Turn off the lights when you leave."

"Will do." Vi's smile was a little too vibrant, like she'd been caught passing notes. "We're almost done anyway."

"Good to hear. You're both doing exceedingly well."

I slapped my hand on the paper. "Thank you, sir."

As the door shut and the Lumsden's footsteps echoed down the hall, Vi let out a long sigh.

"You okay?" I asked.

"Everything's fine." She gave me a look which indicated that fine meant boring. "I like it when there's no drama."

"Hmm." I rested my elbow on the desk and supported my head in my palm. I had nowhere to go, and there was a lot about Vivian Ellis I didn't know. "So, what did you mean when you said if you watched more football you might find a boyfriend who might stick around?"

"You remember that?" She glanced away with a nervous chuckle. "I guess it's pretty obvious. I don't exactly have dudes lined up outside my dorm room door or anything."

I wondered why not. After all, I'd be the first in line if it weren't for my priorities. "That's not an answer. You've got the wares. What is it? Do you prefer not to date?"

"I've dated some, just haven't dated anyone worth keeping around."

Ouch.

"A university of forty-five thousand students, and all the dudes are pathetic?" I asked.

"No, it's not that...um...all the dudes who want to go out with *me* are pathetic."

"Am I pathetic?"

"No."

By the levitating feeling in my gut, I could have floated to the ceiling.

She ground her pointer finger into the desk. "But we're not dating and you've made it clear you're not on the market."

"For now." I bit the corner of my lip. "But I still can't believe there's not someone out there with your number."

"Ha. Maybe one day. I always thought once I went to college I'd meet a guy and fall in love. But here I am, well into my senior year and I'm still single." Shaking her head, she didn't meet my gaze, but clicked her pen three times. "I know it sounds dumb."

"No it doesn't. Lots of people marry their college sweethearts."

Suddenly she took an interest in her fingernails. "Just not us."

I didn't want to let it rest. "But four years and you've had boyfriends, right?"

She shrugged. "Sure, I've dated."

"And now? Have your eye on anyone?"

She closed her laptop, then swiveled toward me, her gaze meandering from my head down to my lap. "No one," she said in a hoarse whisper.

The corner of my mouth ticked up while I slid my hand to her cheek and leaned in, my lips five inches from hers. "Me neither."

My heart skipped at least a dozen beats while I stared at her without blinking, willing her to inch closer.

She widened her eyes behind those sexy glasses. "Why do I feel like you're going to kiss me?"

I grinned. "I think you're going to kiss *me*."

"But I can't."

"Why not?"

"Because you don't want me."

My finger curved around her chin and tilted that delicious mouth upward. "I don't deserve you."

As she began to speak, I took the plunge and showed her exactly how hot she was, sealing my mouth over hers with a searing, tongue-entangling kiss. But this time I made it count. She deserved better, but the mere thought of seeing her with someone else drove me insane.

Moaning into my mouth, she brushed her fingers around my neck and raked them through my air. I needed her so bad, I deepened the kiss, tasting her, devouring her.

And she kissed me back, her hands on my face, her fingernails grazing the stubble that had grown in since the morning's shave. She was too damned far away. I grabbed her gorgeous ass and pulled her onto my lap, needing, wanting, craving to be closer.

As Vi gently eased her lips away, we both were panting. "Does this mean you're on the market?"

I tucked an errant lock of her hair behind her ear. "I think I went on and off in a heartbeat."

"But what about us?"

"Can we take it slow?"

"How slow?"

God, I wanted to unzip her jeans and yank them down to her knees. "Kissing is good," I croaked. When I swore off women, I thought it would be easy. Hell, I thought I wouldn't look at another female for a year or more. But all it takes is one kiss from Vivian and I'm on fire.

"Kissing is unreal. I mean, I'm totally dazed."

"Yeah." Dazed was an understatement. Completely stupefied. Utterly mystified, and absolutely hard as a stag during a rut. I'd been hard for weeks.

Months.

I was so hard it hurt.

Vi scraped clean white teeth over her lip. "You sure I'm not messing with your head?"

"Woman, you've been messing with my head ever since you introduced yourself in the library foyer."

She chuckled deep in her throat, a sexy, seductive sound that made me need her more. "Sounds familiar."

I wrapped my arms around her and buried my face in her neck, wanting to say so much more, but I buttoned my lips. The memory of my trial was still too raw. My fucking mind balanced on the blade of a Samurai sword. On one side there was Vi and sunshine. Heaven help me, there was sex. Or the promise of sex. The mere thought made a bead of come leak from the tip of my cock.

And on the other?

On that side there was an abyss of pain.

But right now, this woman felt so good in my arms, her head cradled in the curve of my neck.

"This is nice," she whispered.

Too nice.

Forcing myself to lean away, I looked her in the eye. "You are amazing, know that?"

"Nah." She adjusted her glasses. "Honestly, I'm pretty ordinary."

"Never say that. No girl I'm into is ever *just ordinary*."

Chapter Nineteen

Vivian

I'd suddenly developed a case of attention deficit disorder as I sat in my Corporate Law lecture doodling daisies and then counting the petals to divine as to whether Cade really liked me or not. An odd number meant yes, an even, no.

At the moment odds were winning three to one.

Yeah, I was being stupid and sophomoric.

Or was I completely insane?

Maybe.

So, now we were officially kissing, but not really dating. Jeez, there was nothing like setting myself up for a major crash and burn.

How many botched relationships had I endured over the past four years? The worst was Ethan in my freshman year. He looked like a nerdy Tyler Posey and I was idiotic enough to worship him. I still can't believe I dated that asshole for a year before I found out how much he cheated.

I did everything for that bastard. I even went on a diet because he thought I needed to lose some weight...while he was cheating on me, with a stick figure from his English class, the utter moron.

Thank goodness he graduated last year and I'll never have to set eyes on his too-cute-for-a-guy face.

Returning to the present, my first clue that the lecture had ended was when everyone started packing up while I still doodled. I had to be losing it. I needed to stop fixating on Cade. Stop kissing him, too.

If I zoned out during another lecture I'd end up failing an exam or at least ruining my A average. Besides, the last thing I needed was to dive into a relationship with the outcome headed straight for a guaranteed heartache. It took me a year to recover from Ethan and between him and my dad, my experience with the opposite sex bordered on catastrophic and pathetic. The only man in my life who had given me any sense of stability was my grandpa.

I grinned. Grandpa was always good at saying the right thing at the right time. I had no idea how he did it...unless he read minds.

As I collected my things and followed the crowd out of class, my cell buzzed with a call from Mom.

I hadn't told her about Cade, only that I'd received a tutoring assignment and it was going well.

"Hi," I said, filing outside and taking the path to the deli where I was meeting some friends for lunch.

"Hey, sweetie. I'm at the hospital with Grandpa and thought I'd give you a quick call."

Stopping dead in my tracks, my heart nearly exploded out of my chest. Did I just think about him because something bad happened? "What hospital? What's wrong?"

"There's nothing to worry about, just some routine tests."

"But where are you?"

"Madison."

"You came all the way to Madison for routine tests?"

"Well, yes. They have the right equipment here."

"For what? Is he okay?"

"He's fine. Groused the whole car ride from Johnson Creek to here. I don't think it's serious. He just has had a rasp in his voice that they want to scope and while they have him here they're doing a colonoscopy as well."

Grandpa had had a rasp for a while now. "Has his voice gotten worse?"

"I don't think so. Like I said, the doctor ordered the tests as a precaution."

"Well, if you're in Madison, I want to see you."

"That's why I called. Do you think you can manage to slip away long enough to come by? They've given him a room. I expect them to wheel him back at any moment."

"Absolutely. I'll leave now. What's the room number?"

"Three-twenty. Third floor. It's the outpatient wing."

"All right. It'll take me about twenty minutes to walk there. See you soon."

I shoved my phone into my pocket and power-walked straight for the hospital. It wasn't like Mom not to tell me if there was a real problem. Surely, she would have. But still, the questions mounted in my mind. Grandpa was seventy-nine and I'd never seen him sick.

Goodness, his forgetfulness was bad enough. Two years ago, he'd sold his house and moved into a facility where they took care of his meals and his laundry and he got to play bingo and watch movies with his friends.

He might be getting old, but I couldn't imagine the world without him. The faster I walked, the more my mind raced with the things that might be wrong. By the time I reached the hospital, I was half expecting to see Grandpa hooked up to dozens of beeping machines.

When I finally found his room, I stopped for a second to wipe my eyes and take a deep breath. The last thing he needed was a hysterical, blubbering granddaughter weeping as if he were on his death bed.

The door was open, so I knocked on the jamb while I popped my head inside, finding only one machine beeping with his vitals. He also had an IV in his arm. My mother sat in a chair holding Grandad's hand. Her face was tired and worn. I swear, more gray streaked through her chestnut hair since summer. When she looked up, she smiled the same smile that always made me warm inside.

"Vivian," she said, making my tension instantly wash away.

"Hey." I tiptoed to the bedside and smoothed my fingers over Grandpa's forehead. "How is he?"

Slowly opening his eyes, he reached for my hand. "At least my nurse is a hottie...could you get her phone number?"

Oh my God, I burst out laughing. Here I was worried sick, and the old man was ogling the nurses. "You think she's sweet enough for you?"

"Damn straight, except her hands are cold."

Mom patted his arm. "You know what they say, cold hands, warm heart."

"So how was the procedure?" I asked. "Any news?"

"They removed a mass from his larynx and sent the tissue to the lab. But otherwise, things look good. Hopefully, that will be the end of it."

I nodded, squeezing Grandpa's hand. He looked so frail in the hospital bed, wearing one of those godawful cotton gowns, the blanket tucked around his waist. The deep lines of his face etched like the bark of an old oak, wizened, weathered. He'd had a long life, yet I didn't know what I'd ever do without him. His wife, my grandmother, had a heart attack fifteen years ago. I was only seven, but I remember how strong he was. How he just kept going.

My throat constricted. I wasn't ready to see him decline. "You know I love you, right?"

"Never doubted it." He licked his dry, cracked lips. "Know what I need right now?"

I shook my head.

"Ice cream," he whispered.

Mom tugged up the blanket. "I don't think that's a good idea. They said fluids only until you pee."

"Do you think I give a rat's ass what *they* say?" He pushed his head against the pillow and looked at me. "Be a champ and go find me some ice cream, Peanut."

I shrugged at Mom. "I don't think it will hurt. After all, it's liquid when it melts."

Her lips formed a line as she gave me a nod.

"I'll be back in a jiff."

The hospital cafeteria wasn't only about a mile of corridors away, when I finally found the place they didn't have any ice cream. The cashier suggested I go across the street to Cold Stone. I thought that was a major score, because if you ask me, Cold Stone has the best ice cream in Wisconsin. I ordered three, Grandpa's favorite, vanilla with a scoop of dreamsicle, oatmeal cookie batter for my lunch, and dark chocolate for Mom.

On the way back, I thought I'd save some time by cutting through the Children's ward, but I ran into an enormous crowd. With cameras flashing and people laughing, I wondered if some celebrity might be visiting.

Until I caught sight of Jason. I shouldered my way forward and saw them all—the O-line as Cade called his gang. They were handing out footballs and teddy bears, except my student wasn't among them.

I would have stayed longer, but my ice cream had started to ooze, so I tiptoed away. Right before I reached the elevators, a child's laughter made me stop. There was Cade, sitting on the floor with a little boy wearing a hospital mask and a blue robe over his standard-issue gown.

I moved behind a potted fiscus tree where I wouldn't be seen.

Cade signed a squishy football and gave it to the child. "Here you go."

"Wow!" The boy's eyes grew as round as silver dollars. "I'm gonna save this forever."

"Where are you going to put it?" Cade asked.

"You kidding? It's going on my bed. I'm not letting this out of my sight."

Cade patted the boy's shoulder he looked so tiny and thin as if he were about to break. "What kinds of sports do you like to play?"

"Football of course. I want to be a tight end just like you."

"Cool. I'll bet you'll be awesome. And practice every day. Do you know what it takes to be the best?"

The boy shook his head. "Nooooo."

"Practice. The more you practice, the better you'll be."

"Then I'm gonna practice every chance I get."

Cade mussed his hair. "That's what I like to hear."

"Jerry," said a nurse who came walking straight toward the boy. "Go and join the other kids."

"But I'm—"

"Go on, quickly now. I need to have a word with this young man."

I watched as Jerry clutched his ball to his chest and cast a forlorn look at Cade.

The big tight end stood and offered his hand, looking like a giant compared to the little guy. "My bros over there are anxious to meet you, too. Catch you later, okay?"

After the boy rejoined the others, the nurse jammed her fists into her hips, her eyebrows slashing downward. "What do you think you're doing, taking that child away from the group?"

Cade spread his palms to his sides. "Beg your pardon ma'am, but I found Jerry here alone. I just stopped to say hi and give him a ball."

"Well, he certainly doesn't need a ball from you. I can't believe they let someone like you interact with children."

"Excuse me," I said stepping out from behind the tree. "But this gentleman was acquitted and is one of the most respectable football players I have ever met."

The nurse glared at me. "I don't care. He is no appropriate role model for any child under my supervision." She turned to Cade, shaking a wicked finger. "I think it's best if you leave."

A tic twitched in his jaw. I'd seen it before. I swear the guy teetered on the verge of losing it, spun tighter than a music box coil. But he didn't say word even though his face had turned fiery red. Heck, if steam came out his ears I wouldn't be surprised. With a sharp nod, he turned on his heel and headed for the stairwell.

"Cade, wait!" I said running after him, bobbling the ice cream.

But he sped up, pushing through the door.

"I mean it!" I shouted as I followed, my voice probably echoing all the way to the operating rooms. "That woman had no right to speak to you like that."

"No?" His footsteps stopped. "Then why the hell do I have to take her shit?"

"I don't know." I stamped my foot, not at him, but because I was so freaking mad. "You shouldn't. She's evil. She doesn't know the facts."

Cade leaned against the wall, balling his fists. "Facts never seem to stop anyone from having an opinion."

"Don't listen to them."

"That's a little hard when they're pointing a finger under my nose and staring me in the eye." Grimacing, he glanced down to my hands. "Why the hell are you here, anyway?"

"Mom called. My grandfather had some tests."

"Oh, man." Cade's shoulders dropped. "Anything serious?"

"Not sure, but if his eye for the ladies is any indication, he's fine."

He pointed his thumb at the cups. "I take it he has a sweet tooth as well."

"The first thing he asked for was his nurse's phone number, the second..." I held up the Cold Stone. "The best."

Licking his lips, Cade almost grinned. It's just his face was too etched with frustration and disappointment to really smile. "Well, enjoy it."

"Why don't you come with me?"

"Nah." He batted his hand through the air. "I don't need another lecture from one more person I've never met."

I raised the cups of melty treats. "Anyone tries that again, and I'll sacrifice my oatmeal cookie batter on their face."

"You'd do that for me?"

"Hey, I'm very protective of my students." I inclined my head toward the stairs. "Come on. Grandpa might bark, but he doesn't bite. Besides, if I stand around here any longer, they're going to be eating soft serve."

"Might as well," Cade mumbled as he followed. "Since I've been eighty-sixed from the children's ward by Maleficent."

Chapter Twenty

Cade

Vivian's Grandpa took a bite of ice cream and gave me a once-over with a furrow etched deeply between his eyebrows. "You play football for the Gyrfalcons, did you say?"

"Yes, sir. I'm a tight end."

"That means he catches the ball," Vi explained.

"I know what it means." Grandpa took another bite. "Aren't you the kid who got himself mixed up in some sort of sex scandal?"

Could this day get any worse? Bitched out by the children's nurse and now pegged for my year of shame by Vivian's grandfather. Taking in a deep breath of air, my gaze shifted to the door. How fast could I escape?

"He was found innocent," Vi insisted as if she needed to defend me.

Those ancient grandfather-ish eyebrows arched. "Are you innocent, son?"

I sidestepped toward the door. "Guilty of being young and stupid but completely innocent of the charges brought against me."

Resting his head back against the pillows, Grandpa's shoulders shook with his chuckle. "Well, I wouldn't mind being young and stupid again."

"Are you happy to be back on the team?" asked Vi's mother, Alice.

Relaxing a little, I shoved my hands in my pockets. "Very happy, ma'am."

"There's a good chance Madison will go to the championships." Vi held up her cup of ice cream. She'd hardly touched it. "Want a bite? It's oatmeal cookie dough."

Any other flavor and I might have said no, but my mouth watered just smelling it. "You sure you have enough?"

"Plenty." She took one more bite then pushed a scoop toward me. "I wish I'd known you were here, I would have bought you one."

Reluctantly, I opened my mouth and let Vi feed me, aware of her mom staring at us. But the moment the flavor burst in my mouth I forgot about any awkwardness. Sweet, cold, creamy. Why was cookie dough always better than cookies? "Whoa."

"Good isn't it?" she asked, holding up another spoon.

"Unbelievable." I licked my lips, dying for another taste. "But don't you want it?"

"You probably need it more than I do."

When it came down to food, I wasn't one to argue. "It's so good. One bite and I'm addicted."

"Are you treating my girl right?" asked Grandpa.

Vi threw out her hands. "I'm his tutor, for heaven's sake."

"You didn't tell me you were teaching a football star," said Alice.

"Excuse me?" Grandpa set his empty cup on the table and leaned forward. "I asked the boy a question."

I cleared my throat. "Yes, sir. Vivian is top shelf."

The old man's eyes twinkled. "You better believe she is."

"So, Cade," said Alice. "You said you were from New Jersey?"

"Yes, ma'am."

"Are you going home for Thanksgiving?"

"I can't," I said, licking my lips. "We have practice the day after and a game on Saturday."

"That must be hard on you, and disappointing for your mother."

I shrugged. "She's used to it by now. The only guys on the team who go home are the locals."

Alice stood and tossed her cup into the trash. "Why don't you come to our house? We'd love to have you. Wouldn't we, Vivian?"

"Uh..." Vi gave me a panicked look. "Sure. That is if Cade doesn't have other plans."

Thanksgiving with Vi's family? I was planning to go to Cruisers with the guys. But getting out of Madison for a day might be okay. I looked to Grandpa. "Will you be there, sir?"

"You kidding? My daughter makes the best stuffing this side of the Mississippi."

I wanted to ask what stuffing he'd had to the west that was better, but I managed to keep my mouth shut. "Sounds like a meal a man needs to experience at least once in his life."

"Wonderful," said Alice.

Vi pointed her thumb to the door. "We'd better get going. I have a ton of homework."

Grandpa reached for her hand. "Thanks for coming, Peanut."

"I'm glad Mom called." She gave him a peck on the forehead. "And I want to know the results of those tests."

After the goodbyes, Vi pulled me out into the corridor. "Sorry my mom put you on the spot. Are you okay?"

I laced my fingers through hers, remembering why I'd ended up in her grandfather's hospital room. "Better. Thanks."

I meant it, too. Getting away from the situation with the nurse and seeing Vi's family totally changed my mood. Had she not twisted my arm, I probably would have gone to the gym and beat the shit out of a punching bag.

"Good." Once we stepped outside, she stopped and faced me. "Don't feel like you have to come over for Thanksgiving."

"You kidding? And miss the best stuffing this side of the Mississippi?"

"Mom's a great cook, but we...um." Vi's gaze trailed aside while a blush spread up her cheeks.

"What is it?" I asked.

"I don't know. We're poor. Mom lives in a trailer. She keeps it tidy, but I don't want you to...you know...feel sorry for us, or be shocked, or stop kissing me because I'm...I'm..." She hid her face in her palms. "Trailer trash."

Reaching out, I rubbed her shoulder. "Is that what you think? I'll judge you because you're not rich?"

With a groan, Vi dropped her hands. "That's an understatement. Dirt poor is more like it. Heck, Mom qualifies for food stamps."

"Do you think I care?"

"I—" She cut off and ran her hands over her head. "I guess I hoped you didn't."

"Well, your mom, who I'll bet is the most awesome mom in Wisconsin, just invited me to Thanksgiving dinner and I'm going whether you like it or not."

"All right, then."

"Exactly." I shook my head. "All right."

"You want to take the bus to Johnson Creek with me, or will you ride your Harley in the snow? You do know it usually snows around here on Thanksgiving."

"The bus might be interesting, as long as I can make it back for practice Friday morning. After practice, the team is heading to Chicago for the game with Northwestern."

"We always eat early—noon at the latest. There'll be plenty of time to get back."

I cupped her cheek and stole a quick kiss. "Thanks. I think spending a little time away from Madison will do me good."

Chapter Twenty-One

Vivian

My lips were still buzzing when I loaded up a tray and met Lisa at the student deli. It was really a cafeteria, but no one used that word on campus. It was definitely taboo with the administration.

Lexi, the bombshell transfer from Milwaukee was sitting beside her. I groaned to myself while the back of my neck prickled. I had absolutely no reason to dislike the girl, even though she reminded me of something out of *The Stepford Wives*.

"I see you two found each other," I said, trying to sound chirpy as I slid into a chair with my tray.

Lexi smiled—a practiced, perfect grin that made me want to barf. "Sure did."

Lisa picked up a packet of ketchup and squirted it on her fries. "She's writing an essay on the Williams trial."

"Oh?" I asked, suddenly losing my appetite.

"I am," the girl purred. "You never told me you're Cade's tutor."

Right. I was supposed to reveal all the facts of my life in the half-minute we talked.

My gaze shot to Lisa, who was putting pickles on her hamburger, not looking at me, and behaving as if Lexi had every right to pry. I shrugged. "It's no big deal. He's trying to get ahead."

"Why would he care?"

"Because he wants to get his degree."

Lexi pursed her lips as if she'd just sucked on a lemon. "The only thing that dude cares about is getting drafted into the NFL."

About now I wished I'd grabbed a piece of lemon meringue pie so I could shove it in her face. How dare she jump to conclusions? "Have you asked him?"

She coughed out a guffaw. "Well, *no.*"

"My advice is before you start forming opinions, it might be a good idea to talk to the dude himself."

"No need. My work is about the trial and the *evidence.*"

"Okaaaaaay," I said, stabbing my salad and shoving a bite into my mouth.

Lisa nabbed a French fry and bit off the end. "Now that you've had a chance to look at the court transcripts, do you agree with the jury?"

Miss perfect tsked her tongue. "The problem is, women are always victimized, no matter what happened."

"And men never are," I mumbled under my breath.

"Clearly you're biased," said Lexi.

I was about to strangle her when Lisa's foot lightly kicked me under the table. Then she arched her eyebrows at the girl. "Why don't you tell us how you arrived at your conclusion? How do you interpret the evidence?"

Moving to the edge of her seat, Lexi whipped her finger through the air as if she were a complete expert. "First of all, they were alone in his apartment. It's a famous football player's word against hers."

Lisa nodded while my blood boiled. "The record says she *claimed* she was too inebriated to make a sound decision."

Hello? Lisa had met Cade—liked him, too. *Why was she being so analytical and unfeeling?*

"Exactly," Lexi stabbed her salad with a fork. "He took advantage of her."

I pounded my fist on the table. "Excuse me? But—"

"And then took her home after which she sent him texts indicating she enjoyed their date," Lisa interrupted, leaning forward on her elbows while I did a fist-bump under the table. "Not to mention, the video evidence from the footage in the defendant's apartment building that clearly showed her in control of her faculties."

Rolling her eyes, Lexi snorted. "How can a video prove how drunk a person is?"

I clamped my hands to my spinning head. I did not want to think of anyone having sex with Cade.

Not ever.

Unless it was me.

And this definitely wasn't the conversation I wanted to have with my dinner. I'd missed lunch and had given Cade half my ice cream. Hell, after witnessing the nurse kick Cade out of the children's ward, I was ready to throw darts at anyone who questioned the man's character. "Look. The jury acquitted. The dean reviewed the evidence and allowed him back in school. Why the hell are you trying to make a sham out of it? Are you looking for some gossip to post on your blog?"

Lexi's eyes widened. Aha. She didn't know I'd checked into the blog and knew it was her. It didn't list the owner, but I'd taken enough programing classes to find out *she* was behind the Gyrfalcon Feathers. And furthermore, her idiotic blog had reported the details of the trial from the day it began.

The girl's surprise quickly vanished as she pursed her lips and gave her shoulders a little self-righteous shimmy. "You'd better watch yourself with that dude. He has bad news written all over his M.O."

In my opinion, the girl across the table was the one with a questionable M.O. My mind shot back to the picture of us in the park and I wondered if she had been following us. Did she take the photo?

Probably.

Well, I wasn't going to buy into her crap. "There's no need to worry about me. But what I want to know is why did the plaintiff go to Williams' apartment in the first place? Why did she send him kissy texts after the event?"

"He coaxed her there after he got her drunk at a party. And she *was* drunk. She told me herself. It wasn't until the next day that she realized how stupid she'd been."

"So, if you purport that the evidence is so cut-and-dried, why did the jury acquit? Why did the dean reinstate?" I shoved my chair away.

"You're just biased."

My nostrils flared. "On the contrary. When it comes down to Cade Williams' character, I think I'm very grounded. I've probably spent more time with him one-on-one than anyone else since his return to school. And I believe he's making every possible effort to focus on his studies and football and nothing else."

"That's true," Lisa agreed. "He even took my roomie to a couple of parties to keep the women at bay."

A cynical laugh gushed through Lexi's nose. "So that's why you were kissing in the park?"

"That..." I stood and picked up my tray. "Was a mistake."

"It was. He was a total dick about that," said Lisa as I strode away and tossed my food into the bin. By the time I reached the door, my entire body was shaking.

Who the hell does Lexi think she is?

And why do I care?

I broke into a run.

God save me, I cared about him. I didn't want to know that he'd had hot sex with some woman who later decided she'd been a victim. I didn't want to know that he'd had sex with anyone.

Did I?

What really happened that night? If he was innocent. Why had the plaintiff changed her mind and then taken her case all the way to court? What did Cade do to make her want to ruin him?

And why the hell couldn't people like Lexi and the nurse at the hospital leave him alone!

I ran up the stairs of all nine floors of my dorm building. Gasping for air, I burst into my room and threw myself on the bed. I'd been pretty damn quick to tell miss priss our kiss in the park was a mistake. Why? What was I afraid of?

Would he hurt me like Ethan had?

I wanted to be with Cade more than anything. But I needed some sort of commitment before I completely gave him my heart. Not a pledge to love me forever, but at least a promise to try. A willingness to take a risk.

We both needed to walk the plank together and either dive to the depths or soar into the clouds.

Dammit! If I had to swear on a Bible, I would have no choice but to admit kissing Cade in after I tackled him topped my list of most epic experiences. My entire body came alive in his arms as if a primitive force deep inside snaked its way to the surface. It was inexplicably powerful.

Until he told me he'd sworn off women for the rest of his life.

Chapter Twenty-Two

Cade

Sitting beside me on the bus, Vi wore a puffy down-filled coat and a striped stocking cap that looked like it came from Santa's Elves. "Are you warm enough?" I asked.

"Mm hmm." Her smile seemed a little reserved. "But you must be freezing. You can't be comfortable in a hoodie."

"You kidding?" I rubbed my chest like the cold never bothered me. "It's supposed to be twenty degrees during Saturday's game. I need to toughen up."

"Right, as if you aren't already a tough guy."

"Hey, it ain't easy getting knocked around every weekend."

"Then why do you do it?"

"I've told you why."

She blew into her gloves while puffs of mist billowed around them. "Yeah, but every time I see you get tackled I practically have a heart attack."

"You're beginning to sound like my mom."

"Ooo." Vi cringed. "I definitely do not want to go there."

When the bus turned onto the interstate it was as if someone released my inner steam valve. In Madison I was always so tense and on guard, waiting for the next person to snipe at me. I checked over my shoulder—fortunately, the seatbacks were so high, the few passengers on the bus couldn't see us.

Yawning, I draped my arm around Vi's shoulders. "I hope you're okay with me crashing Thanksgiving with your family."

"Are you kidding? If you'd said no, my mother would have been totally wounded."

"Well, then I'm glad I'm here. I think."

"Why think?"

"Because I want you to be glad I'm here."

"Of course I am." She looked out the window. Flurries had started. "It's just..."

Something was bothering her and I'd been sensing it for a while now. "Come on, out with it."

"I don't know. I guess things have been so tense lately, I must be de-stressing from all the exams before the break." She sat straighter and took a deep breath. "Don't worry about me. By the time we reach Johnson Creek I'll be ready for turkey."

Okay, I wasn't going to press her. We all had exams and papers we had to write. I leaned my head back and closed my eyes for a while, until another thought dawned on me. "Have you heard about your grandpa's tests?"

"Not yet. Mom said they'd find out sometime next week." Vi's brow furrowed. "I just hope he's okay."

"I'll bet he will be. He seems like a fighter to me."

"Yeah, but he's getting old." She rubbed her hands on her pants legs. "He's always been such a rock in my life. I can't imagine him any other way."

"Then don't. Why worry when there's no need to?"

"Easy to say, not so easy to convince my brain."

The snow outside continued but the bus hurled down the freeway as if it were sunny and dry.

Vi gave me a nudge with her elbow. "I'll bet your mom misses you."

"Yeah." Mom missed Dad more, but she always put on a poker face for her kids. "I had a video call with her and my sisters this morning. At least she has the girls there to keep her busy over the holidays."

"And your game. I'll bet she has never missed one.

"She's my greatest fan." I took off my hat and raked my fingers through my hair. I didn't know what I would have done without her support. "If it weren't for her I would have completely lost it last year."

"You're lucky to have her."

"Sure am." I gave Vi a sideways glance. She didn't overwhelm me with questions like so many others did. Instead, she watched me expectantly, giving me the room to say more but not pushing me. I appreciated that about her. "Mom is another reason why I'm trying not to screw up. My arrest almost killed her. That, on top of losing my father, was more than any woman should have to bear."

"I can't even imagine how much it tore her up inside. She must be strong."

"No one tougher. Did I tell you she's an ER nurse?"

"Seriously? Talk about major stress. Hers must be on a cosmic level."

"Yeah, and it gets worse. She was there the day they brought Dad in."

"Oh God." Vi rubbed her outer arms. "How horrifying."

"But leave it to Mom to put a positive twist on it. She told us kids she wouldn't have wanted it any other way because she got to hold his hand and say goodbye." I barely got the words out before my throat closed.

Vivian's eyes teared up. "That makes my heart twist. She must be something special, I'd say."

I hugged her close, squeezed my eyes shut, and kissed her temple. "Mom says every day is a gift and if we don't take up the reins and give it our all, we only have ourselves to blame."

"I guess there aren't any do-overs when it comes to time."

"None, sweetheart," I whispered, my mouth turning desert dry. I'd never called a woman sweetheart before, but it fit. I liked the sound of it.

Turning her face up, Vi's gaze connected with mine. A crackle of energy pulsed through me as I studied those beautiful brown eyes behind the sexiest glasses I'd ever seen. "Know what I want right now because if I don't ask, we'll miss this moment forever?"

She didn't have to say another word. My heart knew what she wanted. Hell, my entire body reacted like a firecracker. As my lips neared hers, Vi's soft gasp made my heart kick into high gear. And as our mouths joined, she melted in my arms. I'd been hungry for the taste of her for days. She was so sweet, like ambrosia for my soul.

God, I wanted this woman more than anything. My body needed her more than food, water, or the air I breathed. My hand slid around her puffy coat and found her waist. I pulled her closer, craving more.

Craving her.

All of her.

When Vi slowly pulled away, she was panting, just like me. "What is it about you?"

"Me?" I swirled my fingers around her silky cheek. Her skin was so soft, so feminine. "It's all you, babe."

The bus took an exit, drawing Vi's attention out the window. "Oh, we're here."

I craned my neck to look around her. There was a ginormous hardware store across the street, but otherwise it was pretty rural, thick with bare trees, their limbs stretching in all directions as if in a fight to catch the snow. "That was fast."

"I think the time goes faster when you're with someone."

The bus stopped at a gas station and I was surprised to see no one had come to meet us. If we'd been going to my mother's house, she would have been there with my sisters standing in the icy wind holding a welcome home sign. But then Vi didn't go to college out of state.

"Is your house close?" I asked, noticing the snow wasn't sticking to the road. That was great because I needed to take the seven o'clock back to Madison tonight.

Vi pulled me by the hand and inclined her head. "We're in the trailer park just over there."

I checked my six. "So this is the metropolis of Johnson Creek?"

"Postage stamp is more like it." Laughing, she started to run. "What's it like at your house?"

"We live across the river from Philadelphia. There're buildings and concrete everywhere you look."

"Philadelphia sounds so east coast."

"It is." I followed at an easy jog. "Nice city, though. Lots of history."

Vi stopped outside a blue single-wide trailer with planter boxes in the windows. It looked picture-perfect as if the person who lived here took great pride in keeping the place nice. "This is it. Last chance to turn back."

"You kidding? I can smell the best stuffing in the world from here. There's no way I'm heading back to Madison now."

"All right, then." Vi knocked on the door before she opened it. "Anyone home?"

"You're here!" Alice beamed as if she hadn't seen her daughter in months. She even gave me an enormous bear hug.

Inside the trailer was homey and warm with a super small kitchen. I inhaled as I hugged her back. "If dinner is half as good as it smells, I'm going to be in heaven."

Grandpa welcomed us from an easy chair propped in front of the television.

"You got the game on?" I asked, moving to the couch beside him.

The old man's features sagged with his blank expression. "What game?"

"The Packers are playing Seattle."

He handed me the remote. "Jiminy crickets, no one tells me anything important around here. You find the channel, will you son?"

"I'll set the table," said Vi.

I clicked on the game and looked up. "You need help?"

"I can manage. You guys enjoy. Besides, I need to mix up some cookie dough."

"On Thanksgiving?" I asked.

"I won't bake them until after we eat."

Alice popped her head around the textured glass panel partially separating the kitchen from the living room. "Vivian always bakes cookies whenever she comes home."

I licked my lips. "I can't believe my luck. Turkey, the best stuffing east of the Mississippi, and cookies."

Grandpa sniggered, pulling out a tin of chewing tobacco. "You want a pinch?" he whispered.

"I'll pass, thanks."

He pointed to a soda can. "I spit in this. Don't tell Alice. She doesn't like me chewing in the house."

I sat back and settled in to watch the game. "Your secret's safe with me."

Over the next couple of hours, pots clanged in the kitchen, the Packers won, and Alice came in and told her father to throw out that disgusting soda can and if she ever caught him chewing in her house again, she'd set him in a lawn chair beside the road with a sign that read "Free to good home: tobacco-chewing old fart."

After she returned to the kitchen the codger gave me a nudge. "She says that every time."

"You ever think of quitting?"

"You kidding? At my age, a man doesn't have many things that bring him pleasure."

"Even though it's not good for you?" I asked.

"Hell, you sound like my daughter."

The NFL commentators came on for the end-of-game recap and Grandpa nudged me again. "You sweet on my princess?"

Shifting in my seat, my gaze darted toward the kitchen and back. Jeez, Vi was close enough to hear every word I said. "Ah...I'm trying to focus on football and my studies at the moment, but I'll have to admit, teaming up with Vivian is the best thing that's happened to me in over a year."

"You're sweet on her, all right." He sat back and spat into his can. "I have one piece of advice for you, son."

"What's that?"

"You've only got one ticket on this ride they call life, and it's not every day you find a diamond like my granddaughter. Stop dwelling on the past and live your damned life because you never know. Any day could very well be your last."

I stared at him before my head dropped against the couch. What did he know about my life? Or my dad? What would my father have done if someone told him a week before he died that he only had a few precious moments left?

I was still contemplating Grandpa's words of wisdom when Vi stepped into the living room and wiped her hands on a frilly apron. "Dinner's ready."

I noticed Grandpa left the disgusting soda can beside his chair. Maybe Alice's threat to sell him wasn't entirely made in jest.

But dinner was delicious and, though I'd never utter a word to my mom, Alice's dressing was so good it melted in my mouth. My mother always set the big dining table with fine china and decorated the house. Here we were, sitting at a tiny table with four chairs in a trailer house and none of our plates matched. But it didn't matter whether we were at a fancy table with china and crystal wine glasses or using Chinet and glass, the meal was delicious.

Just as I stood to help Vi clean up the dishes, the phone rang. Alice took it in the back room and then returned with her coat draped over her arm. "That was work. Two waitresses called in sick."

"You're kidding." Vi put a plate of leftovers in the fridge. "You know they're not sick. They're just sticking it to you."

"Nonetheless, the restaurant is packed and they're going to pay me triple time." She pulled her keys out of her purse. "Come on, Dad. I'll drop you off on the way."

Vi stamped her foot. "But you need cookies!"

"You're so sweet." Alice smiled and slid her fingers over Vi's cheek. "Leave me some. You pair are still taking the seven o'clock back to school, right?"

Alice opened the door and in swooshed the wind and a flurry of snowflakes. "Yes," Vi replied.

There was about an inch of snow on the ground. "You sure you're going to be all right driving in this weather?" I asked.

"This? How long have you been in Wisconsin?" Grinning, Alice grabbed the handle and stepped onto the deck. "This is a piece of cake compared to what's coming."

I knew it wasn't bad, but still, who wanted to go to work on Thanksgiving when it was supposed to be her day off? "Thank you for the meal. The food was awesome."

"You're welcome, and I hope we see you again soon."

As Grandpa followed his daughter and the door closed, Vi huffed and jammed her fists into her hips. "Those other waitresses are such assholes!"

I agreed with her, but on the other hand we were finally alone.

Off campus.

Turning toward the counter, Vi started putting dollops of cookie dough on a tin sheet. "Well, at least I can ensure Mom will have a nice treat when she comes home."

I studied her ass. God, all I wanted to do was sink my fingers into her soft glutes and pull her against my erection.

But by the way Vi was attacking the batter and ferociously flicking each spoonful, making it splat on the pan, I figured I'd probably end up with a broken nose if I tried it.

"That's super nice of you," I said. "Does she have a thermos?"

"In the cupboard above the oven."

I found it and pulled it out. "We ought to leave this full of hot chocolate with a thank you note."

"She'll like that." Vi put the cookies in the oven, set the timer, and turned with her fists on her hips. "Wait a minute."

Uh oh. What did I do? Rather than come up with something incredibly witty to say, I just stood there like an oaf and said, "Huh?"

"Who are you?"

"Um." I rubbed a hand up my abs. "Same guy you've been hanging out with for the past three months."

"Cripes, it *has* been that long." She turned away and untied her apron, then efficiently folded it and put it in a drawer. God, if it had been me I would have draped it over the back of a chair. "Three months of not-dating, with occasional kissing. No wonder I'm a wreck."

I took hold of her wrist and made her face me. I noticed it on the bus, but she'd just admitted something was wrong. Worse, it reflected in her eyes. She bit down on her lip as if she wanted to talk but couldn't bring herself to form the words.

"I'm driving you crazy, aren't I?"

"Isn't this..." She gestured between us. "Driving you insane? Why are you here? Aren't I attractive enough for you? And why the hell won't you ever say anything about what happened to you?"

Jeez, she'd bottled up a lot.

I moved closer. "First of all, I'm here because I was invited."

"Great." She turned to the sink and started the water running. "You could have lied and said you wanted to spend Thanksgiving with me."

I stepped beside her and craned my neck, moving my face closer and closer until she had no choice but to look at me. "Except that wouldn't have been a lie."

"Right," she said turning the bottle of dish soap upside down and pouring in enough to wash dishes for an entire football team.

I reached in and shut off the water. "And if you ever have any doubt as to how hot you are, I'll be first in line to show you."

"Man, you sure know how to make a girl turn to butter."

Lowering her chin, she regarded me through the fan of her long eyelashes while her tongue tapped her upper lip. I planted my hands on her shoulders and made her face me. Hell, I'd been dying to wrap her in my arms since the bus turned onto the interstate this morning. And I wanted this to be the best damned kiss of her life.

Exercising excruciating self-control, I didn't plunge in and plunder her mouth even though every nerve ending in my body was thrumming on red alert, screaming at me to devour her.

Instead, I lightly brushed my lips across hers. And then I slipped my hands to her hips and pulled her flush against my erection. "This is how much you turn me on."

"I can't win," she moaned, sliding her fingers into my hair and kissing with a mixture of urgency and feral intensity, matching the force of the blood racing through my veins.

I completely came unglued with the urgency of her hands as they roamed across my body, trembling as if she'd been starved for my affection forever.

I lifted her ass onto the counter and she wrapped her legs around me, her crotch hot and tight against my cock.

I'd never been so turned on in my life.

And then the damned buzzer went off.

Chapter Twenty-Three

Vivian

A chill shivered through me when Cade pulled away.

I wrapped my arms across my body as I watched him grab an oven mitt, take the cookies out, and set them on the stove. "They can wait," he said, tossing the mitt aside.

For the first time in my life, I agreed. Normally my OCD self would insist I stop everything and neatly place them in straight rows on a paper towel to cool but, at the moment, that side of my brain was on overload. I was panting. I was shaking. And I was so hot, my body was about to explode.

He fell into my arms and buried his face in my neck. "I want to see you naked."

Oh. My. God.

Yes, yes, yes, yes!

He lifted me off the counter and cradled me in his enormous arms, then headed down the hall while the only sound I managed to make was a guttural moan. "Which one's yours?" he asked.

"First right."

He kicked open the door and together we fell onto my bed—a twin with a pink princess comforter.

God, I swear he didn't even notice. He rolled on top of me, while our mouths fused together in a full-contact, tonsil-probing kiss.

I gasped, hardly able to breathe as his lips trailed along my jaw and down my neck. Strong, masculine hands kneaded my breasts as he shoved up my shirt and dipped his tongue into my naval.

Squealing, I arched my back. "I'm so hot!"

His gaze pinned me to the mattress while his fingers opened the button on my jeans.

"You sure?" I asked, barely able to form the words.

Hovering above me, Cade gripped my hips and stared me dead in the eye. "This can't be about me. The question is are *you* sure?"

I released a stuttering breath, my entire body on fire. "Only if you promise not to stop."

"I'm not planning to unless..."

"What?"

"You tell me to. You are in control, okay?"

"Yeah." I was in about as much control as photon on the surface of the sun. "You want me to sign a release?"

For a split second I thought he might be considering it. But then he grinned. "I trust you."

Good God, those were the most romantic words I'd ever heard in my life. Cade Williams, a man who had been on the verge of having his life ruined by a woman trusted me.

I pulled off my shirt and my bra went with it, dropping somewhere on the floor. Screw my OCD, I didn't even look.

Cade's breathing grew ragged as he licked between my breasts. "You're more fucking amazing than I dreamed."

A gasp caught in my throat as he pressed a finger to my lips then torturously trailed it lower, first circling my breasts before he planted his palm on the opened zipper of my jeans. His tongue slipped to the corner of his mouth as his gaze swept up to mine, his fingers gripping my waistband.

I arched my back, fruitlessly reaching for him as he torturously slid jeans and panties off and tossed them over his head.

Grinning, his eyes greedy and filled with pleasure as they raked down my naked body. God, no one had ever looked at me like that before—with so much desire, so much need, so much yearning. "I never want to stop drinking you in."

For once in my life, I didn't feel like I needed to cover up.

I wanted him to see my body.

And he crawled over me. "Your boobs have goose bumps," He said, taking a nipple into his mouth, and sucking so hard I cried out, squirming beneath him. "Your entire body is erupting."

I shivered even though I was hotter than blue fire.

He licked his way down from my boobs all the way to my thigh, his kisses searing as they connected with my fevered skin. "I think I'm going to explode," I moaned.

"No," he whispered, sounding sexier than anything I'd ever heard. His kisses slowed, torturing me with languid swirls of his tongue. "I want to savor you. I want to make this a moment you'll never forget."

"God!"

I'd never been with a guy like this before—someone who put my pleasure first. And somehow he knew exactly where to touch me, taking me to places I'd never dreamed of. Touching, kissing, caressing, I felt him everywhere.

My skin was alive and Cade had me captured in his spell.

I grabbed his shirt and pulled it over his head, not caring where it landed. "Take off your jeans!"

"Not yet," he growled, his voice hoarse and filled with the same passion thrumming through me.

"Serious?" I asked, my heart racing.

"Once I'm naked, it'll be over before it begins. And I'm making you come again and again."

I dropped my head to the pillows. I didn't always have an orgasm with Ethan. Yeah, I got hot, but sometimes it just didn't happen. And Cade expected two?

"One's enough," I squeaked.

A deep chuckle rumbled from this throat. "I don't think so."

Powerless to argue, I only managed a sensuous whimper.

"That's right, ease back and let me take you to the stars."

I squeezed my eyes shut as he shouldered between my thighs and lapped me. Holy mother, stars shot through my vision. His mouth made magic while his fingers slid inside, working in tandem with his wicked tongue.

Gasping, I gripped the princess comforter in my fists, positive I was about to lose my mind.

Totally out of control, I bucked while noises I'd never heard before choked in my throat.

Then suddenly I went completely stiff, sucking in a breath as if it were my last.

And then an orgasm crashed over me like a tsunami colliding with the shore, making my entire body shake. My mind refused to focus.

I kicked.

I screamed.

I yanked his hair so hard, he cursed.

When I finally opened my eyes, his jeans were flying through the air.

Just when I thought I might start breathing again, my gaze focused on him. A totally naked, unequaled, nude man—sculpted like a Greek God.

"Holy. Fucking. Hell," I swore, drinking every inch of him in. God in heaven, if I thought he ought to be on a TV show for America's most gorgeous before, I knew it now.

Laughing, he crawled up beside me. "I didn't think you swore."

"Not usually, but this is the first time I've ever seen perfection...in my bedroom."

Cade wasn't only huge, every muscle in his body rippled as if he didn't possess an ounce of fat.

I smoothed my fingers down his ripped abs, his skin softer than I'd imagined. "You. Are. Gorgeous."

"That's my line." He nuzzled my neck and slipped a tiny packet into my palm. "I need to be in you."

After he watched me slide the condom over him, he took my hands and held them over my head. "Are you ready for number two?" he asked, his lips brushing mine.

A tear slipped from my eye. How had he done it? How had he made me want more?

"Please," I whimpered.

"Are you sure?"

I pulled his mouth to mine and showed him how ravenous I'd already become.

He started slow, sliding into me inch by torturous inch. I watched his eyes glass over and my passion spiked, needing him all the way inside. I sank my fingers into his ass and demanded more. In a heartbeat, my single bed was creaking as we launched into a flurry of searing kisses and mind-blowing thrusts.

"I'm close," I gasped.

"Let it go!" he growled through clenched teeth. "I'm not leaving you behind."

His tongue swept into my mouth while he met the demands of my hands. As I cried out, sailing over the edge again, an ocean of pleasure burst between us. His entire body convulsed as I went limp, clinging to him for dear life.

When our breathing began to ebb, he dropped onto the mattress beside me.

I rolled to my side and toyed with his hair. There were so many things I wanted to say, but the biggest question on my mind was what now? Would things be different when we returned to Madison?

Afraid and unwilling to ruin everything, I kissed him. "Want to have a shower?"

He grinned. "Is it big enough for both of us?"

Chapter Twenty-Four

Cade

Trailer showers weren't exactly manufactured with a man my size in mind. But I figured it might make sex even more fun.

I was already rock hard as I stepped through the glass door and pulled Vi in with me. Sprayed by warm water, I tilted my head back and moaned, letting rivulets stream down my chest.

"It feels good."

I pulled her against me. "You feel good."

Her chuckle rumbled through me. "I can barely move."

"We don't need much room," I said, pouring body wash across the swells of her breasts. "You have the sexiest curves I've ever seen."

She eyed me as if she didn't quite believe it.

I rubbed my cock against her while the suds bubbled between us. "See what you do to me?"

Shuddering, she slid her arms around my neck and kissed me. "Why am I so attracted to you?"

"Don't know." I licked the tender skin behind her ear. "But I'm glad you are."

As our mouths fused in an erotic dance, she swirled her hips in a mind-blowing rhythm.

"Are you ready for me?"

She buried her face in my neck. "Mm hmm."

I sank my fingers into her soft, tantalizing ass and lifted her onto me.

Gasping, she arched, taking me completely inside her. "I'm too heavy."

I bent my knees and thrust. "Not for me, babe. Just wrap those slick pegs around my waist and let me make love to you."

A spark flashed through her eyes while her legs clamped around me. "Yes, yes, yes!"

Rather than utter another sound, I fused my mouth with hers as she hung on for dear life, her hips rocking, milking me, demanding more. I tried to hold back, but the tame accountant turned into a wild woman, demanding deeper thrusts. Just as I didn't think I'd last another second, she threw back her head and spasmed around me.

With one more thrust, I lost it, pulling out just in time, coming into the spray.

***

Before the water turned cold we managed to turn off the shower. Never in my life had I ever been so into a woman. I have no idea how we ever worked up enough self-control to put our clothes back on.

Vi hung up the towels so perfectly, they looked like a department store display, then we dressed and headed for the kitchen. "I'd better finish baking the cookies so they'll be done by the time we have to catch the bus."

Suddenly reality returned like a sucker-punch between my eyes. I checked the clock on the wall above the sink, and then released a relieved breath. It was only five-thirty. Plenty of time.

Vi got to work, scooping dollops of batter onto the sheet. I stepped behind her and kneaded her shoulders.

Rolling her head back, she moaned with pleasure, making me consider hauling her to the bedroom and going for another round. Too bad there wasn't enough time. "Your muscles are tense."

"They're always tense."

"Why?"

"I guess I carry life's stressors in my shoulders."

I kissed her neck, making goosebumps pebble her skin. "What stresses you most?"

"Plenty."

"Try me."

"My mounting debt, finishing school, getting a job after I graduate, Grandpa's health, Mom living alone and being a waitress. Heck, I've never seen her date. She doesn't have a life."

My mom didn't either. She buried herself in work and my sister's lives. "But what else? I often sense you're stressed out about something. And my guess is it isn't everyone else's problems."

Vi turned with a spoonful of dough and pointed it under my nose. "Like I said, I worry about a lot of things, none of which I can figure out right now."

I scraped the chocolate chip concoction off the spoon with my teeth and let my eyes roll back. "Mm. If the cookies are half as good as the dough, I don't think they'll last."

Vi put the sheet in the oven then picked up one from the first batch. "Try."

I bit into it and let the cookie melt on my tongue. "Wow, that's so good."

"Best recipe ever."

"Forget accounting, you could make a mint selling these."

"Right, just like Mrs. Fields and a gazillion other cookie startups."

I grabbed another and ate it. "Seriously, I've had a lot of chocolate chip cookies and these are the best. Just don't tell my mom."

Vi crossed her heart. "Your secret is safe with me."

When her phone rang, I slid onto the living room couch.

"You're not serious!"

The tone in Vi's voice caught my attention. Was it her grandpa?

"How much snow has fallen in the last few hours?" she asked.

I jumped up and looked out the window, cupping my eyes to the glass.

"That must be a record," Vi continued.

Holy shit, four to five feet had fallen while we were...

"Closed?" Moving toward the door, Vi flicked on the outside light. Jeez, the snow was all the way up to the top of the trailer's steps. "Even the freeway?"

I pulled out my cell. Before I unlocked with my fingerprint, "winter warning" flashed up. I clicked on the report. Damn, a rogue storm had unexpectedly blown down from Canada, and we were expecting six to seven feet.

Feet!

My thumbs flew over the keyboard as I brought up the Metro website.

"*All busses cancelled until seven o'clock Friday morning.*"

Shit!

I brought up Uber.

"*Due to storm, all cars are off the road between Milwaukee and Madison.*"

Vi stepped beside the textured glass panel and gaped at me. "I—um—guess we didn't notice the blizzard."

I told her about the buses and Uber. "I'm fucked."

"Didn't you say the local players all go home for Thanksgiving?"

"Yeah." I hung my head. "I shouldn't have come."

"Right. I forgot. You can't have any fun because football and grades are the only things that matter."

The old twitch came back. "Don't razz me."

"I'm not. I'm just saying the entire state is on lockdown. The roads are closed. My mom can't even drive seventeen miles from Watertown." She grabbed my hand and pulled me onto the couch. "But she said the news is reporting the roads ought to be plowed by morning. Text your coach and tell him you'll be there asap."

She made sense, but it still didn't allay the fact that I'd let everything slip.

Because of a girl.

A beautiful, mega-smart, awesome girl. But all the same, Vivian had messed with my focus.

Big time.

"You gonna be all right?" she asked.

"Sure."

She picked up the remote. "Let's watch a movie. There's no use stewing over an act of God."

I took in a deep breath and rubbed my forehead. "Okay, as long as it's got bad guys who get nailed in the end."

"I'm sure Netflix has just thing."

Damn, damn, damn. I could barely sit still. After all that had happened, how could I take my eye off the ball? I'd let my freaking guard down and allowed myself to make love to the woman I'd been dreaming about for months, and there I was, stuck in the middle of nowhere in a blizzard.

Regardless, Coach will fucking kill me if I don't make it by the time the team bus leaves for Chicago.

"I swear I'm going to hightail it back to Madison in the morning if I have to hijack a snowplow."

Chapter Twenty-Five

Vivian

I drummed my pen on the desk in the tutoring office, watching the clock. It was two minutes after seven. Two minutes since our session should have started.

I was a wreck.

I'd hardly heard from Cade after we returned from my mom's. Thank goodness the plows had been out all night and we were able to catch the early morning bus back to Madison. He made it in time for practice and to catch the team bus to Chicago, but he'd tensed up as soon as we got news of the storm.

And that was the end of the hottest date I'd ever had in my life. We freaking fell asleep in the living room watching Disney movies.

I knew how much football meant to him, but it wasn't as if we'd left the country for the holiday. We were a little over an hour outside of Madison was all. I'll bet Cade's coach was snowed in as well. Everyone knew the dude lived out in Verona. He would have had to wait for the roads to be plowed, too.

Worse, the Gyrfalcons lost their game on Saturday and I knew better than to try to talk to him. The players always took losses hard, and I wouldn't be surprised if Cade took it the hardest. They'd only lost one other game this year, and when Monday came that time, my student had been withdrawn and quiet. Fortunately, his moping had only lasted a day.

I stopped drumming and threw my pen across the room. Why hadn't he at least texted me? Now we weren't only kissing, we were having sex. Mind-blowing, awesome sex. And I wasn't the type to have a snowed-in fling and pretend it didn't happen.

Cripes, it was five past now.

I picked up my phone to text him when the door opened.

"Hey," I said, pretending I'd just been looking at something riveting on my screen.

"Hey," he clipped, sitting in a chair but not dragging it beside me as he usually did.

"You okay?"

"We lost."

"Yeah. But it was close."

"No one cares about close. We just blew our chance at the Rose Bowl."

"Oh." I started clicking my pen. The newscaster had said the Gyrfalcons would still get a good bowl placing—

maybe even the Orange Bowl, which I Googled and discovered it was going to be played in Orlando. Heck, I'd love to go to Florida in January.

Nonetheless, the tension Cade brought into the room was enough to squash any happy thoughts that might have popped into my mind.

He leaned forward, resting his elbows on his knees. "It was all my fault."

"Excuse me?"

"I fucked up. I should have caught Devan's pass in the end zone."

I rubbed my eyes and thought back. In the last play of the game the quarterback had thrown a Hail Mary right into a sea of jerseys. So many players tried to catch the ball, but it was too high. Cade had jumped the highest and it had barely missed his fingertips.

Didn't he realize the ball was uncatchable? All the announcers had said so. I couldn't keep my mouth shut. "You might have caught it if Devan wouldn't have overthrown the ball. You sure jumped higher than everyone else."

"Not high enough." He slammed his fist on the desk. "Anyway, what would you know about it? You don't even like football."

I gasped, blinking like I was sitting across from the Hulk. "Excuse me? I watched the damn game. Enjoyed it, too. And if it weren't for you, I'd still be happily doing yoga or reading a book, or anything aside from watching you lose to stupid Northwestern."

Oh. Shit.

I covered my mouth, hardly able to believe what I'd just puked out. I mean, I meant everything I said, but the way it came out sounded nasty.

Cade's eyes flashed wide, then narrowed as if he were about to shoot darts out of his pupils. "Fuck you!"

My breath caught in my chest and speared me. What was I to him? A sleazy one-night stand? I might have been about to apologize, but screw that. Shaking, I stood and started shoving my stuff into my backpack.

He grabbed my wrist. "What the hell are you doing?"

I twisted my arm away. "I'm leaving."

"But we have a session."

"Not tonight. And I'm not about to stay here and listen to you swear at me."

"Come on." He slapped the chair. "Let's do this."

"Do what? Kiss? Fuck on the desk?"

His mouth dropped open as if he didn't believe me capable of fighting back.

Well, he had another thing coming.

I gave him a laser-eyed glare of my own. "That's right. It's okay for the wounded tight end with the tight ass to screw with his tutor, but as soon as the heat turns up, the star player morphs into a total asshole."

He shoved his chair back and threw his arms out. "What are you talking about?"

"You really want to know?" I fumed. "Why don't you ever tell me what happened? Are you pushing me away because of her? Because of some psycho bitch who tried to ruin your life?"

My every word amped up my anger. Slinging my backpack over my shoulder, I jutted my face into his. "Well, I'm. Not. That. Girl!"

Turning, I grabbed the doorknob and yanked it open. "Cripes, you needed me to fend off chicks. You don't care about me. All you care about is your stupid goals!"

"Vi!" he yelled, his voice muffled by the door slamming.

A miserable tear streamed from my eye as I ran down the hallway and pushed outside. Why in God's name did I let myself get mixed up with bad-boy Cade Williams?

He didn't care about me.

All he cared about was a dumb game and acing his next exam.

Chapter Twenty-Six

Cade

I dropped my towel and ran my fingers along the football-sized bruise on my hip and hissed. Getting knocked around usually didn't bother me but I guess I'd taken more than my share of hits in the game against Northwestern.

I'd been pushing hard in practice, too.

Especially after fucking everything up with Vi. I hadn't been to a tutoring session since the day she walked out. A whole week without breathing her in. A week without hearing her sultry laugh. Seven days without kissing her.

Screw it.

I could study without help.

The problem?

I didn't want to. Every time I opened my book, I heard the lull of Vi's voice. Even if accounting was the dullest subject on the planet, I paid attention when she taught it. Hell, the scent of coconuts and mangoes even lingered on the pages.

I forced myself to look at the waiting ice bath and raked my fingers through my hair. Was I really in enough pain to endure eight minutes freezing my nuts off?

I took a step forward and everything ached as if I'd just celebrated my ninety-fifth birthday.

"Just get in," said Jason, pushing through the glass door.

I snorted. "Easy for you to say, bro."

"Ya think?" He stripped off his shorts and took the plunge. "Ahhhhh. Reminds me of Alaska."

I hit the timer and lowered myself into the tub beside his, my balls instantly squeezing, the tension shooting all the way up through my throat. "You've been to Alaska?" I asked, my voice cracking along with my testicles.

"Nah. It's on my bucket list, though." Jason, glanced over, his lips blue and quivering. "Maybe I'll go up and wrestle a grizzly."

I just shook my head, gripped the sides of the bath and closed my eyes.

And there was Vi.

Except she wasn't smiling. Nope. Her face was contorted with anger as she spewed the words that had haunted me for the past week. *"As soon as the heat turns up the star player morphs into a total asshole."*

And she'd been right. I was so focused on the game, I wasn't only screwing things up for the team, I'd screwed everything up between us.

"So, you ready for Saturday?" Jason asked.

I sucked in a deep breath, doing my best to hide the storm brewing inside. "Always ready, man."

"That so?"

I glanced over at my bro. Instead of his usual cocky smirk, he eyed me, his lips pressed together in a grim line. I pretended not to notice. "Nothing's changed."

"Then why are you stampeding through practices like a bull in a fighting arena?

"Stampeding?" I asked, trying to sound like I didn't have a clue what he was talking about.

"You know what I mean. You're trying to kill everything and everybody."

I clenched my fists, my jaw twitching. "Shut up."

"You shut up. You need to cool your jets. You go out there with murder on your mind and you'll get called for offensive pass interference or, worse, ejected from the game for unnecessary roughness."

I didn't reply. I just gritted my teeth and focused on how great it was going to feel when my balls finally slipped back into my nut sac.

"What happened with the tutor?" Jason continued to dig. "Didn't you go to her house for Thanksgiving?"

"She's not the problem."

"Right. She didn't mess with your head. I might believe that except you were almost human before you left campus on Thanksgiving."

Rubbing my forehead, I took in a deep breath before I replied. "And then we lost to Northwestern."

"Old news. I don't need to tell you rule number one. We can't let the last game fuck with our heads. You know the drill—focus on the next game, and the Minnesota linebacker who's going to try to feed you your lunch."

I tilted my head back, noticing one of the overhead lights was on the blink. "Like I said. Nothing's changed."

"Good, cause both of us need to be in the zone, man." Jason's alarm buzzed. He jumped out of his tub and grabbed a towel. "We already lost out on the Rose Bowl. Let's not screw up our chances for the Orange. Got it?"

"You can count on me."

"That's what I wanted to hear."

My alarm sounded next and I smacked it off, then waited until the door closed behind Jason before I pulled myself up, my entire body feeling heavier and more tired than it had before the ice. Maybe I was pushing myself too hard. Even if I were, I couldn't stop now. What about my goals? What about giving two hundred percent for my dad? Didn't I owe it all to him?

I toweled off, but chills still pulsed through me, the words of another man who'd recently entered my world ringing in my ears, *"You've only got one ticket on this ride they call life, and it's not every day you find a diamond like my granddaughter. Stop dwelling on the past and live your damned life, because you never know, it could very well be your last."*

Vi's grandpa had asked me if I was sweet on his granddaughter. Hell, he knew I was.

Of course I was.

Who wouldn't fall for perfection? God, the girl had everything from brains, to boobs, to bloody decency. She wasn't out to date a guy with a price tag attached to his forehead.

But what if things blew up with her like they had last year?

For sure, Vi had made it clear she wasn't like the bitch who'd tried to ruin my life.

And deep down I knew she wasn't. But she didn't understand how terrified I was to start something serious again.

I shivered.

Did I just admit to being terrified?

God, I was so fucked.

Chapter Twenty-Seven

Vivian

Lisa pulled on her Gyrfalcon sweatshirt and gaped at me through the neck hole. "Come on, it's the last home game of the season."

Her father had come up from Chicago with a few clients and Daddy had rented an entire box.

Sitting on the floor with my laptop balanced on my knees, I mindlessly flipped through Cosmo's online magazine in a paltry attempt to focus on anything except the stupid game. "You've sure turned into a football maniac lately."

"And you haven't?"

I pretended to study an advertisement for a pair of ridiculous-looking platform shoes that I would never wear unless I was dressing up as Lady Gaga for a Halloween party. "I've suddenly lost interest. But what's up with you?" I asked.

"Um…" Turning her back, Lisa headed for the bathroom and flicked on the light. "I might have gone on a date with Jason."

My computer dropped into my lap. "What the hell? And you didn't tell me?"

Lisa returned, shaking her brush at me. "It didn't seem like the time. And besides, it wasn't that big of a deal. We just went to an on-campus movie."

"What movie?"

"*Letters to Juliette*." My suddenly insane roomie bent over and brushed her hair. "And he might have kissed me."

I set my laptop aside. "A kiss and it wasn't a big deal?"

Lisa straightened, pulling her hair into a messy ponytail. "I don't know, nothing happened after."

"Why, because he needed to get up early for practice before classes?"

"That's what he said."

I hopped to my feet and grabbed a bag of microwave popcorn. "Because he did. The players hardly get five minutes to themselves."

Was I jealous? *Hell yeah*. Cade had never even asked me to go to a movie. Jeez, we'd never been on a real date. "Did he say anything about Cade?"

"Only that he knew he hadn't gone to your tutoring sessions all week. And…"

"And?"

"Jason wanted to know what you did to their star tight end because he'd been acting like a complete jerk-wad since he got back from your house."

I opened the micro and tossed the bag inside. "Oh, right. So it's all my fault."

"I never said that."

Jamming my finger on the popcorn button, I wanted to scream. "Cade probably did."

"So, what happened between you two?" Lisa pressed. "I want all the deets here. We have no secrets between us and your lips have been buttoned up for too long."

I climbed onto my bed and flopped on my back. I'd been tight-lipped about Thanksgiving because it was torture to talk about it. "May as well spill it all..."

I told her about Mom getting called to work and the dynamite sex. "I mean dynamite, blow me all the way to the moon type of sex. Sex I'd never even dreamed of before."

"That's insane. If it was that good, why did he diss you?"

"Who the heck knows? After we took a shower, Mom called from the restaurant and said she was snowed in and had to stay up in Watertown, then we found out the bus was cancelled and we were snowed in, too. Next thing I knew, he totally freaked out because he wasn't going to be at practice at first light the next day."

"They practice in six feet of snow?" she asked, hollering above the popping.

"Practice was in the gym and then the team bus was scheduled to leave for Chicago Friday afternoon since the game was Saturday morning."

"Did he miss the early bus?"

"No, silly." The microwave dinged, but I ignored it. "When we woke up, the snowplows had been running all night and the roads were clear enough for the buses to start up. We caught the seven o'clock back to Madison and I'll bet he made it to practice by nine-thirty."

"You don't know for sure?"

I slapped my hands to my forehead. "I haven't had a chance to ask."

"So, you had awesome sex, and then he freaked out because he thought he might miss practice and maybe even an uber important game?"

"But we checked the forecast. I knew he'd just be a little late at the worst. But, oh no, that wasn't good enough for him."

"Unbelievable," Lisa huffed.

"You know he has these goals. Things he has to prove because of his father." I held up my finger. "Did you know his dad was shot in a convenience store robbery?"

"God, I'd forgotten about that. But Vi, isn't that enough to mess with anyone's mind? And then he spent a year fighting a bogus case that—"

My stomach turned over. "That he refuses to talk about."

"He's probably still wallowing in PTSD. I swear, the guy has to be scared shitless."

"Afraid of what?"

"You!" Lisa pulled the closet door open. "I'll bet sleeping with you freaked him out more than being stranded in the snow overnight."

She pulled out one of my Gyrfalcon sweatshirts and handed it to me. "Put this on."

My brain was too overloaded to argue, wondering how on earth Cade Williams could be afraid of me. I pulled the sweatshirt over my head. "You mean, my affection caused him to lose it and give me the silent treatment all week? Why the hell didn't he say something, rather than let me think I was the worst sexual partner on the planet?"

"Who knows? You're not exactly an experienced hussy."

"Shut up."

"Sorry." Lisa ducked back into the closet. "I shouldn't have said that."

I don't think I turned him off—*Did I?* It seemed so intense. The bedroom, the shower, the counter...

"Just take my word for it. He's got a shit-ton of baggage he needs to sort through and you just walloped him with more. And need I say that dudes are terrible at expressing their emotions?"

True. At least I'd had enough botched relationships to figure that one out.

Lisa came out with my coat and threw it over my face. "Come on. Don't make me go to my dad's stuffy business meeting alone."

"It's not a business meeting."

"Seriously, dude?" She tugged me by the hand and dragged me to the door. "My father will seal more deals today than he has in the last month."

While we were waiting for the elevator, another problem popped into my mind. "You know that chick, Lexi?"

"Don't remind me," Lisa scoffed. "Now she knows we're roomies, she won't shut up."

"About Cade?"

"Yeah, she's obsessed likes she's on some sort of vendetta."

"I think you're right. I wish there were a way we could get the school to shut down her blog."

"Huh?"

I looked up at the numbers, floor five, six... "She's the one behind Gyrfalcon Feathers."

"Oh, right, the blog that posted photos of you and Cade in the park." The elevator doors opened and we stepped inside. Lisa pulled up the blog on her phone and gaped. "My God, where the hell did she get this bullshit?"

I leaned in and read the headline. *Madison's Most Notorious Tight End Should be Behind Bars!* I wanted to puke. "Can she libel him like that?"

Lisa pocketed her phone. "I'm not a pre-law major for nothing. Let me do a little digging."

***

Being enclosed in the luxury box above the stands was surreal. Though now that I was here, I wanted to be closer to the field. I wanted to be in the cheap seats with the students so I could jump up and down and scream my head off.

So far away from the field, I found it difficult to keep my eye on the ball. I always seemed to follow the quarterback's fake, and then had to watch what actually happened on the instant replay on the screens above the window.

"How do you like Madison?" asked a middle-aged executive who wore too much aftershave.

It was halftime everyone was refilling their drinks and loading their plates with spinach puffs and fried cheese curds. "It's awesome. I wouldn't have gone anywhere else."

"I've heard only good things."

I took a sip of my sparkling water. "Do you have a kid who's interested in the school?"

The guy turned red. "In fact, I do. My son will be a senior next year."

"Does he play football?"

"Lacrosse."

I knew we had a lacrosse team, I just couldn't say if it was any good. "Cool."

I moved away from Mr. Chatty and returned to my seat, pretending to take keen interest in the marching band so I wouldn't have to make small talk. I had way too much on my mind to be sociable.

How did I feel about Cade, really? I mean, it was hard for a girl *not* to fall for a guy who looked like God's gift to the female race.

Especially when she was his tutor and shut in a ten-by-ten office with him four nights a week.

Especially when said stud was such a good kisser.

And turned out to be a sex fiend.

A gifted one at that.

Had I fallen under his spell? Heck, I was a serious student with a solid future ahead of me.

What was I thinking falling for a guy with so much baggage?

I expected better from myself.

Right?

On top of everything else, he was probably going to go pro.

What then?

He'd dump me for sure. And if he didn't, everyone knew the pros had women chasing them all the time from professional cheerleaders to professional street walkers. It had to be a nightmare for the girlfriends and wives.

Falling in love with Cade would only set me up to get hurt again.

I should be happy he dissed me.

But I'm not.

For the past week, my chest has felt like a pile of bricks has been crushing me.

And what if Lisa was right? What if he hasn't come to a tutoring session because he's freaked out?

I leaned forward as the Gyrfalcons ran out on the field with Cade, Devan, and Jason in the lead.

The game was tied and the guys were playing their best. Even Lisa's dad said so.

"You ready for the second half?" she asked, sliding into the seat next to me.

I clamped my arms around my stomach to stop the churning. "Nervous."

"Me, too." She set a glass of wine on the table between our luxury leather seats—it was totally cushy and posh in the box. But I still wanted to be down in the student section. "I nearly had a heart attack when Jason caught that ball and was tackled from behind. It looked like the dude hit him so hard he got whiplash."

"I thought he'd fumble for sure."

"But he didn't, thank God."

My mind rifled through a number of plays where Cade had been savagely pummeled. Sure, Jason got tackled, but Cade always seemed to be in the thick of every play, taking the brunt of the hits.

After the kickoff, I shook my head as the Gyrfalcon offense took the field with Cade lining up. Yet another reason to count my blessings that he'd dissed me. If we stayed together I'd be a nervous wreck during every game.

If only he weren't so hot.

Or smart.

Or funny.

Or interesting.

Or full of surprises...

By the time the clock had wound down to three seconds left in the fourth quarter, I couldn't remember any of the reasons why I ought to stay away from him.

Everyone in the box was on their feet. The game was tied *again*, we had the ball but were too far away to kick a field goal.

"It'll go into overtime for sure," said someone behind.

"The next play will be the last—there's not enough time for another," said Lisa's dad.

Clenching my fists, I pressed them against my lips. "Come on guys."

Madison broke from the huddle and all the players headed for the line of scrimmage with no one behind the quarterback.

"Oh my God," said Lisa. "They're going for it."

My fists moved up higher, smacking the bottom of my glasses.

With my next blink, Devan fell back while a linebacker on the other team ran straight for him.

"No!" I shouted, my stomach flying to my throat. Devan scrambled, weaving under the linebacker's tackle. He took two steps and hurled the ball down field.

Oh, God, there were a sea of mixed uniforms in the end zone.

Just like the Northwestern game, it was anyone's ball.

My heart lurched. What if a Minnesota dude caught it and ran the ball back for a touchdown? Why the hell were they taking this risk when the game was set to go into overtime?

I held my breath as the ball sailed over helmets and fingertips, straight to the corner of the end zone.

Then I gasped like I'd just been shot.

Cade jumped so high, his thighs were even with everyone else's helmets. With the tips of his fingers, he trapped the ball and pulled it into his arms just as a defender hit him from behind. Somersaulting through the air, time slowed as he curled his knees to his chest and sailed downward.

As he landed on his back, I heard a sickening thud all the way up in the heated box. God, he hit so hard, his head whipped back and slammed into the turf.

Not once.

But twice.

My jaw dropped. By some miracle he'd managed to stay inbounds, his arms clutching the ball.

"How in the hell did he do that?" someone said as I stood there stunned.

They'd run the same play against Northwestern and Devan had thrown the ball too high for Cade to catch it. Lord knew, the big tight end wasn't going to let that happen twice.

The entire stadium erupted in earth-shattering cheers. Even in the luxury box everyone was on their feet, jumping up and down, shouting at the top of their lungs.

Except me.

Cade still lay on his back while the ref pried the ball from his arms.

"Get up," I growled through clenched teeth, chills firing across my skin.

But he didn't move.

The Gyrfalcon medics ran onto the field, surrounding him until the only thing I could see were Cade's cleats.

"Pleeeeaaaase!" I shrieked.

"That tackle probably knocked the wind out of him," said Lisa, the tremor in her voice deceiving her worry.

I gasped when Cade's helmet rolled out of the mob. And the longer the medics stayed on the field, the more my nerves frayed.

Until an ambulance drove onto the field.

"No!" I shouted while a medic placed a cervical collar around Cade's neck.

"My God," Lisa whispered, clutching her fists over her heart.

I made a dash for the door. "I have to go down there!"

"You'll never get past security," Lisa's dad grabbed my elbow. "I'll text my driver and let him know you need a ride to the hospital. He's waiting outside the main gate—a black Mercedes limo."

I gulped, my gaze darting to the field. They already had Cade on the stretcher. My best chance of getting to him was to take the ride.

"Thank you!" I cried, running out the door.

Chapter Twenty-Eight

Cade

Would they stop poking me already?

I've been x-rayed, MRI'd, CT-scanned, and every inch of my body has been examined by a doc with ice-cold hands. I swear, if someone tried to shove a probe up my ass I was going to get violent.

"I'm fine," I mumbled while a nurse injected something into my IV. I took in a breath, making my ribs feel as if I'd been stabbed.

What happened?

I wasn't stabbed, was I? I think I was at the game...

"This is for the pain," said the nurse, her voice sounding like she was in a tunnel. "We'll have you up to a room in a few minutes."

I tried to push myself out of the bed. "Hell, no. I'm walking out of here."

She shoved me back with one finger like I was a kid, the movement making my head throb. "What do you think you're doing? You have a concussion."

"I'm fine," I insisted.

She snorted. "And I'm Madonna."

I wanted to argue more, but whatever she gave to me was hitting my bloodstream big time. My eyelids drooped. God, I was so tired, but I didn't want to sleep.

I caught the ball, God dammit. If only I could focus, I might remember what happened next. Did I hear a whistle?

No.

Shit.

But I caught it. I know I did. And I needed to get out of here so I can get in shape for the bowl game.

I hope Vi was watching.

But why would she? I'd treated her like crap.

I tried to open my eyes, but my lids felt like they had fifty-pound weights attached to them.

All right. I'll just have a little shuteye. Afterward, I'll head straight to her dorm and apologize. I don't care if I have to camp outside her door while all the chicks on her floor take shots at me. I'm going to apologize like a man. Yeah, she might slam the door in my face. She might even slap me. God knew I deserved it.

I didn't deserve Vi.

But I wanted her.

Hell, I wanted that woman more than football.

My eyes suddenly flashed open, then drifted shut.

Had I actually admitted such a thing? Am I delusional?

At my side, I splayed my fingers just to ensure I wasn't dreaming.

Nope. At least I was conscious enough to know this past week had been hell. Why had I stayed away? Why couldn't I let go of the past and look to the future?

My bed started moving and I opened my eyes again.

"Awesome catch, dude," said the orderly.

"Thanks." I grinned. Yeah, I scored. Now all I needed was to score with my tutor—make her realize I wasn't an entire lost cause. I just had some rough edges.

My thoughts rattled around in my head the guy pushed me into an elevator, up God knows how many floors, then pulled a couple of left-hand turns.

"Here we are," said the orderly, steering the bed through a door and making my head spin.

I tried to raise up, but it was useless. I was wiped and I couldn't fight it anymore. I just let everything go black.

***

Warm, pillowy soft lips caressed my forehead.

Please, God, let it be Vi.

But no matter how much I tried, I couldn't open my eyes. "Is that you?" I asked, but the sound came out like a cackling whisper.

"Cade? Are you awake?"

My prayers answered, I managed to raise my lids enough to peer through slits. "You're here."

"Of course I'm here." She ran her cool fingers across my forehead and I opened my eyes a little further. Her hair was a mess, her glasses smudged, and she looked like the hottest dime I'd ever seen.

I ran my tongue over dry, cracked lips. "You're so gorgeous."

"And you have a concussion."

"So they told me." I tried to push myself up, only to be stabbed in the side. "Ow."

"You also have three fractured ribs."

The air whooshed from my lungs as I remembered I was in a hospital room. "Say, what?"

"Sorry, I thought they'd already told you."

Maybe they did. "They gave me something for the pain. It knocked me out." I shook my head, only to make it throb. "I need to get out of here. Got to get ready for the bowl game."

"I don't think so. Because you have a pretty serious concussion, they're keeping you here overnight. Besides..." Vi's gaze trailed away.

"Besides what?"

"First of all, the game isn't until after Christmas."

A lead ball formed in my gut. "Is there a second 'of all'?"

"I shouldn't be the one to tell you, but yeah. You can't play with three broken ribs."

My life flashed before my eyes. If I couldn't make the bowl game, I'd have to come back to Madison for another year—deal with all the bullshit. Worse, Vi was graduating. She wouldn't be here.

I lay back and stared at the ceiling. She wouldn't want to hang around and wait for me. "Fuck."

"Sorry," she whispered. "But your catch was nothing short of a miracle."

"I guess that's what they mean by taking one for the team."

"You said yourself football is risky. That's why you're studying so hard."

I pursed my lips. Hell, I didn't expect this. No bowl game? Another year getting badgered by all the maniacs who didn't accept the jury's verdict?

I didn't think I could take it.

Vi squeezed my hand. "Look, I know it's a lot to process at the moment, but it isn't the end of the world."

"Maybe not for you. I—"

"He's awake," said a nurse from the doorway. "Do you feel well enough to take a call from your mom? She's worried sick."

At the moment I didn't want to talk to anyone, not even Vi. "Sure."

"Okay, I'll just transfer the call."

Vi squeezed my hand again. "Do you want me to wait out in the hall?"

"Maybe you should leave," I said as the phone rang so loudly it rattled my brain. I pressed the heels of my mands to my temples. "God damn!"

"Hello?" Vi answered. "Yes, he's right here."

She handed me the receiver. "It's your mom."

The poor woman must have had a heart attack. "Hey."

"Oh, sweetheart, it's so good to hear your voice. How are you?"

"I'm okay. I'd be better if they'd let me out of here."

"The doctor said he's holding you overnight. Now don't you worry, I'm working on getting a flight out in the morning. Can you believe that? There isn't one until tomorrow!"

"No, Mom. You don't need to come. I'm okay."

"Excuse me? You were carted off the football field in an ambulance. Of course you need me there."

I glared up at the ceiling. This was a disaster. "You know the docs. They're always overreacting."

"It didn't look like they were overacting to me."

"Yeah, but I'm feeling fine," I said while I was positive the room had started spinning. "Besides, my girlfriend will nurse me back to health. And I'll be home in a few weeks. You know that."

"The girl you went to Thanksgiving dinner with?" Mom asked, sounding uncertain. "Are you sure?"

"Positive. You stay there and look after my sisters, okay?"

"Well, if you think it's best. But the girls can always spend a few days with Aunt June. All you need to do is pick up the phone and ask me to come and I'll be on the next available flight. Okay?"

"Okay, Mom. I love you."

"I love you, too. And son..."

"Yeah?"

"That was the most heroic catch I've ever seen."

I grinned. Even though I felt like shit and my entire life was sinking down the drain, my mother had a way of making things better. If only for a second. "Thanks. I needed that."

Vi was still standing by my bedside when I hung up the phone. "Girlfriend?" she asked. "That was quick."

"I just didn't want Mom to come out."

Judging by the purse of Vi's lips, I should have owned up to the fact I was head over heels. Only, this didn't seem like the time. She crossed her arms. "You could probably use her help. At least for a couple of days."

I closed my eyes. "Maybe."

There was so much to say, but too many things had suddenly changed. I needed to think and to do that I needed to be anywhere but in the hospital.

I can't miss the bowl game. I just can't!

Chapter Twenty-Nine

Vivian

When the elevator dinged outside Cade's apartment, my stomach erupted with a flurry of butterflies. I knew it was him.

My palms perspired as I turned in a circle, suddenly feeling like I was trespassing.

Should I hide?

Gah! What a stupid idea. I moved behind the kitchen's breakfast bar and folded my hands, watching while the lock clicked and the door swung open.

Cade stood in the hallway and gaped at me. "What the hell?"

I cringed, wrapping my arms across my midriff.

Jason came into view behind the big guy. "Whoa. I've never seen this place look so superb."

If only Cade appeared to be half as impressed as his friend, my throat might not be closing at the moment. "Um, I just thought you might want to come home to a clean apartment," I said, though I had no idea it would take me an entire day to tidy up, including hauling five garbage bags down to the dumpster. "I also hope you don't mind that I baked cookies."

The guys came in and Cade nabbed a warm one from the breakfast bar. "You didn't need to go to so much trouble."

"I knew you liked them and wanted to do something—" I was going to say "nice", but Cade had obviously tuned me out as he headed for the bedroom.

Jason pulled up a stool and helped himself to three cookies. "The place looks seriously amazing. You want to come clean mine?"

"No thanks," I said, crossing my arms and peering expectantly down the hall.

"Hey, don't mind him, he's just got a sore head."

"Literally."

"He took the news hard, you know. My poor bro has the worst luck of anyone I've ever met. Even once he clears concussion protocol, Coach won't let him on the field with broken ribs."

"I didn't think he would."

Cade reappeared. "Stop talking about me like I'm some kid who can't handle his own shit." He flopped onto the couch, the movement making him grunt like a wounded bull. "And I don't need babysitting."

I picked up a cookie and considered throwing it at him, but that would mess up all my work. "Who said anything about babysitting?"

He gave me a stink eye.

I grabbed a paper towel, wrapped a half-dozen cookies in it, and handed the bundle to Jason. "Would you mind leaving us alone for a while?"

"I don't mind, but are you sure you want to hang around with him? I can handle the ogre for a while if you want."

Shaking my head, I gestured toward the door. "I'll call for back up if needed."

"Okay. You have my number."

I waited until Jason left before I took the plate, put it on the coffee table, and took a seat beside the grouch.

"The place looks nice," Cade said as if it was painful to pay me a compliment.

But I had to give him the benefit of the doubt. His head probably hurt. And I'd cracked one rib before. Just breathing hurt like holy hell, and Cade had fractured three.

"Thanks," I replied. "It was pretty messy."

"Yeah. I wasn't expecting to have a guest."

They'd released Cade from the hospital under the proviso that he'd have someone with him for the next forty-eight hours as a precaution. And I guess I was stupid enough to volunteer. "I'm not exactly a guest."

"No."

"You're stuck with me."

He flicked the channel. "Got any milk?"

"As a matter of fact, we do. The fridge is full and we're having tacos for dinner."

"Jeez, you don't have to cook."

"What? Would you prefer Chinese takeout?"

He looked at me as if I were a complete stranger. "I would prefer it if you weren't here."

I drew in a sharp breath.

God, that hurt. Stabbed me in the gut. Made me want to double over and bury my face in my hands. Instead, I stared at my clasped fingers and tried to convince myself not to take the plate of cookies and throw them in the trash. I wish I hadn't bothered to bake them.

It couldn't be easy. Right? I know he didn't want to come back to Madison for another year, but I figured it wasn't the end of the world if he did. Though I knew he'd worked out his schedule to have enough credits to graduate in the spring. Still, plenty of players enrolled in graduate classes for their last year of eligibility, especially guys who redshirted in their first year. Jason told me during the hours we'd sat beside Cade's bed in the hospital.

But nothing mattered right now, except we needed to get along. I'd agreed to stay, but I wasn't going to be punished for it. "Let's get one thing straight. It's not my fault that you're hurt. I am here because I care about you and I made a commitment. I, for one, keep my commitments, but I will not be the butt your whipping post. Got it?"

He gave a nod.

"Good." I grabbed my backpack and moved to the breakfast bar. I had plenty of homework to keep me busy, even though being here ripped my heart to shreds. Cade didn't care about me. It was over between us. Hell, I guess it was over before it began.

In the hospital for a minute, I thought he'd been glad to see me—that was until he got the news that his football days were over for the year.

Well, I'd just fulfil my obligation and move on.

I had plenty of worries of my own like finishing school and testing for the CPA exam.

***

To the tune of the news starting on the TV and my stomach growling, I checked the time on my computer. I'd been working for the past two hours and Cade hadn't said a word. He hadn't moved, either.

I glanced at him over my shoulder. "You hungry?"

"I guess." He shrugged. "Um, what happened with your grandpa's tests? He okay?"

The dude was wallowing in so much self-pity I was almost surprised he remembered. "The mass on his larynx wasn't cancer, but they're still going to remove it so it doesn't try to take over his throat." I tried to keep the emotion out of my voice, but the news was a huge relief. I'd planned to tell Cade at our first tutoring session after Mom gave me the news...if he'd shown up.

"I'm glad."

"Are you?" I asked, moving around the breakfast bar and opening the fridge.

Cade didn't say much while I cooked dinner. He also opted to eat on the couch. I didn't join him.

Clearly, he was drawing a line in the sand. Whatever his future might be, I wasn't in it.

Chapter Thirty

Cade

The next day I awoke to the smell of crackling bacon. My stomach growled and my mouth watered. More than anything, I wanted to get out of bed and chow down.

But I didn't.

Vivian had been unbelievable. For the love of God, the woman had cleaned my apartment. And it was repulsive—*dude* repulsive. I don't think I'd had time to push a vacuum around so far this year.

Gross, I know. But when a bro is taking double his class load and trying to be the best tight end in the country, there's not much time for housekeeping.

I draped my arm over my eyes. She ought to leave. I needed my space and, besides, if I told her how I really felt about her, I'd just be setting myself up for a crash. Come May she'd be out of here. No way she'd hang back with a loser.

"Cade, breakfast is ready," she hollered like my mom. Or my wife.

As I rolled out of bed and headed for the toilet, it hit me.

Wife.

Never, ever had I remotely thought any woman sounded like she could be my wife. Now I knew I'd hit my head so hard I was delusional. What the hell would I do with a wife? I needed to obliterate that thought right out of my brain. I was dirt poor and on scholarship. Most of all, if luck reared its ugly head and turned against me next year, there was no way I'd make it to the pros.

What then?

Fall back on my education and take an eight-to-five like everyone else?

Be a high school coach like my dad? I could live with that. But Vi deserved more. She deserved to be treated like a queen—not saddled with an unlucky slob like me.

I bent over the sink and studied my face in the mirror. I wished one day my luck would change. Why always me? Why did my life have to be so hard? None of the other guys had to sit out a year because of a psychopath. None of the other guys had to commit to repaying a gazillion dollars in legal fees just to prove they were innocent.

Why couldn't something come easy for once?

Hell, Jason has sailed through his college career. And Devan? He's up for the Heisman this year.

Me?

My ribs hurt so bad I was barely able to suck in a breath at the moment.

It just isn't fair.

I brushed my teeth, splashed some water on my face, then sauntered out to the kitchen.

Hell, I went weak at the knees. Vi looked hot—I swear her hair was all wild and sexy even when she crawled out of bed. She smiled—a sad smile. "Good morning."

"Hey." I said, sliding onto a stool. "You didn't need to fix breakfast."

Vi set a cup of coffee in front of me followed by a plate of eggs, bacon and an English muffin with butter oozing off the sides just how like it. "Maybe not for you, but I like to eat well."

I took a sip. Damn, even the coffee was good. She was too wonderful. Too nice. And I had no idea why she chose to hang around me. I dipped my muffin in the yolk and took a bite. Yeah, the food had to be good, too. "So, why are you still here?"

Vi pointed at me with a crispy slice of bacon. "Didn't I make myself clear last night? Regardless of how much I want to leave you to wallow in your misery, I promised to be on concussion watch."

Ouch.

But she ought to dish out far worse. I've been behaving like an utter jerk. "Unfortunately, I'm not going to die of a brain hemorrhage, so I release you of your commitment."

Turning to the sink, Vi twisted on the hot water and poured a shit-ton of soap in the frypan. "Okay."

Okay? What was that supposed to mean? I shoveled food in my mouth while I watched her whole body shake as she fiercely scrubbed the dishes. "You always put in so much effort?" I asked. "Maybe you ought to go out for the football team."

She slammed off the water and threw a sponge, hitting me between the eyes. "I thought you were a fighter," she shrieked, her eyes wide and piercing like lasers.

"What the hell are you talking about?" I shouted even louder.

"You're sitting there feeling sorry for yourself like a wimp. I thought you were the kind of guy who looked adversity in the face, grabbed it by the neck and beat it down."

A flame ignited in my chest and burned like a bitch. "I am a goddamned fighter. I've proved that every day since I came back to Madison." She didn't have a clue what it was like listening to students whisper hateful shit while all I wanted to do was pay attention to a boring lecture.

Vi reached across the breakfast bar, grabbed the sponge, and squeezed it. "Yeah, except now that the heat's really cranked up and the fire is burning your balls, you're acting like a total whiny dick."

Where the hell did she come up with that line of bull? What did she know? I sure as hell wasn't going to take it. "Right?" I bellowed. "And you'd never cut yourself a little slack after breaking a few ribs and watching your year flush down the toilet." I slammed my fist on the counter. "And don't tell me you wouldn't. You have no idea what it was like to come back here and put up with all the hate—the bastards are out there needling me with their passive-aggressive whispers every singled damned day."

Vi crossed her arms, her face turning red. Hell, she was so pissed her eyeballs bulged. "Well, I'm not a hater. I'm a *stayer*. But you obviously don't want me. And you're obviously never going to tell me why I'm not good enough for you!"

She ran to the bathroom and slammed the door.

Stunned, I sat there like a dope. For fuck's sake, the awesomest woman I've ever met had slept on my couch, made me breakfast, and I'd just ripped her a new one.

I had to be the sorriest asshole on the planet. My throat closed as I listened to her sobs.

Shit.

What was I thinking?

I'd hurt her. All because I was so damned disappointed with myself.

Not good enough for me? Too good was more like it. She'd said it, Vi was a stayer. I mean, we'd had the most explosive sex of my life. Worse, afterward I'd acted like a jerk and the woman still didn't bolt. She didn't try to claim that I'd assaulted her. She just carried on like we were a normal boyfriend and girlfriend.

Normal couples had their ups and downs. Maybe she knew me better than I knew myself.

I hung my head. Could I pull it together and trust her? Hell, if I couldn't trust Vivian Ellis, there's no one on the planet I could trust. And right now, I was the lowest, most miserable jackass. No matter how pissed I was about my damned luck, I needed to face her and let her know exactly how awesome she is.

I took my pathetic butt to the bathroom door and twisted the knob. Damn, she'd locked it. Pressing my forehead against the wood, I sucked in a cautious breath, making my ribs hurt like a sonofabitch. "I'm sorry. You're right. I'm a total fuckup."

"I didn't say that."

"Well, you should have."

She blew her nose, then it sounded like she'd put the toilet seat down. Was she sitting?

"Come on," I said. "Unlock the door."

"Leave me alone."

I pushed my back against the far wall, slid down to my ass, and stared. "Not a day goes by I don't relive the nightmare."

Vi's crying ebbed, though she had a hiccup with each breath. But the woman deserved the truth. Even though it was going to kill me to say it out loud.

Before I started, I blew out a silent whistle. "One of the party girls—you know the type—had been playing me for a while. I liked her, I guess, and asked her to go to a concert.

She wore a skirt that barely covered her ass..." In the mosh pit, she'd stood in front of me and urged me to finger-fuck her. At the time I was so damned turned on, I'd nearly come in my jeans, but I was too ashamed to admit any of that to Vi.

When no comment came from the other side of the door, I skipped over the sleazy stuff and continued, "Things got steamy. We came back here and had a good time."

"A-as good as the time we had at Mom's?" God, she sounded so uncertain.

"Nowhere near as good as that." I gulped. Things had been off the charts with Vi. Real. "She didn't want to stay. I took her home and kissed her goodnight. Later she sent me some lovey-dovey texts—which ended up being a big part of my defense. But anyway, when I left her at her door I thought everything was cool between us. Until..."

"Until what?"

"Until her friend came on to me at one of Devan's parties. Uh...I guess I should tell you that was the next day."

"Her friend?"

"I was dumb. I was thinking with my cock."

"So screwed her friend the day after you had hot sex with the mosh pit flooz?"

"Didn't get that far...but the next thing I knew, I was arrested and charged with sexual assault. And the charges were backed up by the friend. There was even a bruise on the flooz's hip."

"D-did things get that rough? Um...when you were having, you know..." Vi asked.

"No chance."

"She accused you of causing a bruise you didn't inflict? You're kidding?"

"No. In fact I would pay a gazillion dollars to be kidding."

"That's ridiculous. I get a bruise on my hip sometimes when I go to the bathroom in the middle of the night and run into the baseboard of my bed."

I chuckled. It was hard to believe, but now I'd told the story, I felt as if a huge weight had been lifted. "During football season I have so many bruises there's no use counting."

Vi sniffled and blew her nose again.

"Anyway, what happened to me... Well, I'd never admit this to anyone else, but it's made me terrified of..."

Her footsteps shuffled, coming closer to the door. "Of?"

I gulped against the sudden stickiness in my throat. This was the part I hid from everyone... "Women."

"Including me?"

"Especially you."

When Vi gasped, I placed my palm on the wood, imagining her doing the same. "Why?" she whispered.

I ran my tongue across my bottom lip. I'd started now, I might as well bare my soul. After all, I've already been to hell. If she laughs in my face, I guess the devil will welcome me back. Besides, I'm no coward even though I've been behaving like one.

"Because..." I took a deep breath, making my ribs sear with pain. "Because when I look at you I can't breathe. When I look at you, my pulse races so fast, I feel like I've just run for an eighty-yard touchdown."

I hesitated, trying to imagine her face. Hell, maybe it was better if I couldn't see it. "God, Vi, every time another guy looks at you I want to bury my fist in his snout. I want to be with you.

"Kiss you,

"Have you,

"Make love to you,

"I want you to be mine..." I swiped a hand across my mouth and whispered, "*Forever.*"

When the lock turned, all the air whooshed from my lungs.

And then Vi slowly opened the door.

We stood there for a moment, staring at each other, her face splotchy from crying.

Did she totally hate me?

I spread my hands to my sides. "All I can say is I'm so sorry. The last thing I ever wanted to do was hurt you."

Her face split into an enormous grin as she stepped out and wrapped her arms around me.

I couldn't help my grunt as my ribs crunched.

"Oh, God!" She released me, but I'd already closed my arms around her.

"No," I said. "I don't care if it hurts, I want you too much."

"You mean it?"

I pressed my lips to her forehead and squeezed my eyes shut. "Yeah."

With the crook of my finger, I tilted her face up. "Forgive me." Not allowing her to respond, I clamped her face between my palms and kissed her, savoring every second, every sweep of her tongue and the womanly sigh that tumbled through me.

Vi cupped my cheek. "It would have been a lot easier if you'd just put your feelings out there from the beginning."

I gulped. "I just couldn't."

"I know."

But I still had more to say. I had to get it all out before we went any further. "You're graduating. And next year, I'll be back here, I guess."

"Hey, I might be graduating, but there's no reason I can't find a job in Madison." She threaded her fingers through mine and tugged me toward the living room, but I didn't budge. "Look, you're on concussion watch and no matter how much I want to strip you bare and have my way with you, your ribs are too tender for sex, so let's talk. Okay?"

I smirked with a snort. "Sex sounds better."

"As soon as you're able to take a deep breath, dude."

"You underestimate my pain tolerance."

"Serious?"

I slid my finger along the scooped neckline of her t-shirt. "Me on top?"

Vi's lips twisted as her gaze traveled down my body, stopping at the outline of my erection beneath my jeans. "I don't think—"

I pulled her toward the bedroom. "You can overthink these things. Just feel."

Chapter Thirty-One

Vivian

Cade propped the pillows against the headboard, sat back, and tugged my hand. "Straddle me."

No matter how much I wanted him, I still wasn't convinced this was a good idea. "You sure?"

"I know what I want. The question is, do you?"

He didn't have to ask again. I slid my leg across his lap and pressed my palms against the wall. "You okay?"

"Never better." His gravelly response sent chills up my spine as he closed his hands over my breasts and kneaded. With my moan, my hips rocked forward. Cade was my elixir and I'd gone too long without making love to him.

It took two seconds before my breathing sped. He tugged up my shirt, wincing as his arms raised. I took charge and pulled it the rest of the way over my head, letting it drop to the floor.

"Fuck," he growled, pressing a kiss between my breasts as his hands continued to knead me into a frenzy of want.

Arching my back, I unfastened my bra and he yanked it off, his mouth never leaving my skin. With his finger, he traced a line down the center of my body, stopping at the waistband of my leggings. A wolfish grin slowly spread across his lips as those ice-blue eyes looked up at me. He didn't need to speak. I knew what he wanted and it took about a half a second to tear them off along with my panties and then I was on my knees, straddling him again, pulling his t-shirt off him.

He braced his hands on my hips slipped his tongue into my bellybutton. "God, the things I want to do to you as soon as I am able to move."

I froze. "Does it hurt too much?"

"Not so much when I'm sitting up like this." He bit down on his lower lip, pressing his palm against my belly. "I can't stop staring."

"I can't stop feeling."

"Then don't," he said, cupping my butt. "Ever since you hiked the ball in the park, I've dreamed of having this ass in my mouth. He licked his way down the side of my hip.

"You're killing me," I groaned.

"I want to savor you."

I shoved my fingers into his hair. "I want to feel you inside me."

"Protection..." he mumbled. "Side drawer."

"I started taking the pill."

"For me?"

"Yeah. After Thanksgiving."

"You're amazing," he whispered as his hands inched toward my core. I couldn't think, not when his fingers combed through my pubes.

I rocked my hips forward as he slid a finger over my clit. "God. I can't do slow right now."

He chuckled, sliding a finger inside me. "You're hot."

I swirled my hips, craving more. "I'm on fire."

Before I totally lost it, I rocked back and tore open his jeans, shoving them down to his thighs, his erection popping out and tapping his ripped abs. I wrapped my fingers around his shaft and his eyes rolled back. "Your touch makes me want to explode."

"Now," I said. "We can go slow next time."

He grasped my hips and moved me over him. "Please."

It was a request and not a demand. I knew no matter how much he wanted to thrust inside me, he wouldn't do it. Cade reserved that right for me, respected me, showed his love for me. Bracing his cock in my hand I slowly slid down his length, swirling as I lowered, milking him. Our gazes locked, my lips parted. I wanted to watch him as he came to climax.

Careful not to wrap my arms around him and crush his broken rips, I pressed on his massive shoulders while his hands urged my hips up and down, faster and faster. The table beside the bed shook. The alarm clock dropped to the floor.

Unable to stand another second without kissing him, I devoured him with kisses as I matched him thrust for thrust.

Cade's tongue slipped into my mouth, dipping, swirling, licking as a sea of pleasure exploded between us. Throwing his head back, his entire body spasmed as my inner walls quivered round his cock.

Only after my breathing almost returned to normal did I trust myself to speak. "That blew my mind."

"Me, too," he croaked, then pushed the sweaty hair away from my face as his eyes grew hungry again. "Ready for round two?"

***

The next couple of weeks passed in a blur of steamy nights, followed by intense days studying for finals, until Christmas break. There was no way Cade could get out of going home for the holiday, so I spent it with Mom and Grandpa like I always do. I met him at the airport on New Year's Eve and the two of us celebrated in his apartment with a bottle of champagne and a pizza with the works.

The next day we cuddled together on the couch to watch the Gyrfalcon's bowl game with hot chocolate and popcorn. Cade was bummed that he missed out on the trip to Orlando, but ever since the pandemic, the team had stopped allowing players on the injured roster to travel. Though after five days of being apart, I was glad to have him back. His ribs were healing, too, though I was pretty sure he was in more pain that he let on. After all, the doctor said he needed to rest for six weeks and recommended not being on the receiving end of any more tackles until spring training started.

Being a football novice and sitting beside a player who lived and breathed the game was surreal. It was hard to wrap my mind around half of what Cade was saying, but I knew enough to realize, he'd called every play before it happened. And by the fourth quarter, the dude wanted to be on the field so badly, he was ready to jump out of his skin.

When there were three seconds left, the score was tied and he looked at me, his eyes half-crazed. "I should be there."

I pressed my lips together, knowing that stating the obvious would do nothing to calm him down. He'd been jolting, his fingers shaking with every play and it only got worse as the game progressed.

"Does it come down to the seconds like this most of the time?" I asked.

"The good ones do." During the commercial break, he picked up a pencil and a tablet. "Devin has to throw a Hail Mary pass into the end zone, or they're going into overtime." He drew the O-line. "As soon as the ball is snapped, Jason and Gary—the two wide receivers—will take off."

He drew arrows all over the paper as if I had a clue what he was planning. "Since I'm not there, they'll send the running back down field as well."

"Do they have a chance?"

"With my bro Jason out there? You bet."

When the game came back on, Cade jumped to his feet. "See? They've lined up exactly like I said they would."

"I'm almost afraid to watch." I clapped my hands to my face and peered through my fingers. My heart was thumping like I'd run a mile, my nerves on edge mostly because Cade's intensity was totally infectious.

Cade called the cadence with Devan. As the center hiked the ball, Cade sidestepped, throwing his hands up, as if he were really out there. Just as he called it, the receivers and the running back raced down the field while Devan threw a bomb—straight into the hands of the opponents. And if it weren't for the quarterback sacrificing himself, the dude would have run all the way for a touchdown.

Wincing, Cade grabbed his side and slid back onto the couch.

"You gonna live?" I asked.

"Yeah, that last play reminded me why I'm here and not with my team."

Coming back from yet another commercial break an announcer appeared. "The Gyrfalcons sure are missing their tight end, Cade Williams who's out with three fractured ribs and a concussion."

He threw a pillow at the TV. "I'm finished with concussion protocol, you dweeb."

Needing something to do, I snatched the pillow off the floor and hugged it over my stomach. "At least they recognized the fact that you're on the injured list."

As soon as the words left my lips, a replay of Cade's amazing catch in the Minnesota game came on the screen. "Look at you!" I said, thrusting my finger at the picture. "You are a complete and total beast out there."

Cade sat back and laced his fingers behind his head. "It was okay, I guess."

"Okay? You not only sacrificed yourself, you won the game."

"There's a lot more to that play than my catch. First of all, the O-line had to keep the Marmot's defense from busting through and nabbing Devin. Not to mention, my man also had to throw a wicked pass—one that only I could catch."

"With your fingertips, mind you...while a sea of enemy players surrounded you. I think I would have wrapped my arms over my head and run for home."

Cade slid his arm across my shoulders. "Know what I adore about you?"

"My glasses?" I asked, pushing them up my nose.

"They're cute, but when we first met you didn't know jack about football, and now here you are sitting with me, telling me about the winning play of my last game, and you know what the hell you're talking about."

I batted my eyelashes. "Aw, you know how to charm a girl."

In the end, we won in overtime and Cade and I took an Uber to Cruisers for a works burger.

Chapter Thirty-Two

Cade

I gave the bartender a high-five, ordered two specials, and took Vi back to the booth. "I'll bet it was torture sitting out the game," the man said, putting two glasses and a pitcher of beer on the table. "This one is on the house."

"Thanks, bro. You're the best."

"Yes, thank you." Vi shrugged out of her coat and pushed it aside.

"So, how are you ribs?" the man asked.

"Better than they were a few weeks ago. Pretty soon I'll be able to take a deep breath." I looked to the empty booths. "I'm surprised there isn't a crowd."

"There was, but everyone headed home after the game was over."

"Which is why we showed up now." I slung my arm across Vi's shoulder. "It was torture enough to watch the game in my apartment, but it would have killed me to hang with a bunch of fans."

"Damn shame you had to end up hurt at the end of the season."

"It's a shame he had to get hurt at all," Vi said, pouring the beer.

"I'll get those burgers started for you."

As I watched the dude walk away, my phone buzzed.

Vi leaned in. "Who's that?"

"No idea." I didn't recognize the area code but pushed the green button all the same. "Hello?"

"Is this Cade Williams?" came a deep voice from the other side.

"Yes," I said dubiously, wondering if I should have let the call go to voicemail.

"I'm from the commissioner's office."

My mind blanked, wondering which commissioner...and then it dawned on me and I started to sweat. My heart thundered into hyperdrive. "You mean the *NFL* commissioner?"

"That's the one, son."

Vi shoved her face in front of me, mouthing, "*What?*"

"Yes, sir," I said, turning away.

"How are those ribs of yours?"

"On the mend. Doc says a few more weeks and I'll be ready for any Hail Mary pass Devan can throw at me."

"Good to hear. We thought a few broken ribs wouldn't sideline a guy like you for long. What do you say about coming to the combine in April?"

"Me?"

"We've already established that you're Williams, right? Hell, just today I've fielded calls from about a dozen scouts making sure you'll be there."

"Yes, sir. I'll be there and ready to handle anything they can throw at me."

"Awesome. We'll be in touch with the details."

"Thank you, sir. I won't let you down, sir."

"I didn't think you would," he said before clicking off.

"What was that about?" Vi asked, her eyes round as quarters.

I was shaking so badly, the phone slipped out of my hand. "Maybe I won't be doing another year at Madison after all."

"Huh?"

"That was the NFL commissioner's office. They've officially invited me to the combine."

"Which is?"

Vi was such a quick study, it was easy to forget that she knew next to zilch about football. "It means I've been invited to test with the elite college players in front of a boatload of pro scouts." I scraped my teeth over my bottom lip and looked her in the eye. "It also means I have to declare for the draft. No one goes to the combine and stays in school."

"But what about your ribs?"

"It's not until April. I'll be as good as new by then. Besides, we just run routes and that sort of thing—no tackling. As long as I can keep up with sprints and in the weight room, I'll be ready."

"My God—things change so fast with you." She slid down in the seat a few inches. "You're not going to be here next year?"

I moved my hand over her fist, which I realized was clenched tight. I pulled it to my lips and kissed her fingers. "I'll probably get drafted."

"You mean like a first or second rounder?"

I couldn't help but laugh. "Maybe. If I'm lucky, but I'd take any round they gave me."

"And then you'll be gone?" she whispered.

I pulled her hand over my heart. "Not without you...*I hope*. I mean, can't you find an accounting job anywhere?"

She tried to tug her hand away, but I wouldn't let go. "We're a team, right?"

Chewing the corner of her mouth, she glanced aside. "But what about all the women who throw themselves at pro-ballers?"

I opened her fingers and pressed her palm against my heart. "Hey, there's only one woman I want throwing herself at me, and she's sitting right here."

"You mean it?" she asked, looking me in the eye.

"I don't want to have to go anywhere without you at my six."

She leaned in and nibbled my ear. "What about your twelve?"

"You take any and all the numbers you want, babe."

The burgers arrived. Vi stared at hers for a minute. "I'm think I'm in shock. I need time to cogitate. It's April, right?"

"The combine is in April and the draft is in May. And with my load next semester I'll graduate with you, sweetheart."

She picked up her burger and the bacon and egg fell out. "We walked in here with a plan, and after one phone call, the whole world turned on its head."

Chapter Thirty-Three

Vivian

The second semester started in a whirlwind. I applied for and received two new tutoring assignments and, if I hadn't started living in Cade's apartment, we would have crossed paths about once a week. He was busy with his extra load of classes, bound and determined to graduate in the spring.

Toward the end of one of my CPA test prep lectures, the door swung open and Lisa barged inside. Her gaze swept across the faces until she found me and beckoned with a wave of her hand.

"May I help you?" asked the prof.

"Vivian is needed...*um*....now!"

All heads turned my way as I closed up my laptop, slid it into my backpack, and hastened out the door as fast as I could. "What's up?"

"Remember I said I would look into Lexi's blog?"

A stone the size of my fist sank to the pit of my stomach. "Oh shit."

"That's an understatement." Lisa pushed out the door. "We've got to hurry."

Prickles of alarm fired over my skin. "Why?"

"She's staging a demonstration outside the gym."

I felt the color drain from my face and Lisa grabbed me by the wrist while we ran past the Medical Sciences building. "Don't worry. I've already notified campus police."

As we turned the corner, I couldn't believe it. A circle of girls holding placards over their heads had Cade surrounded and backed against a wall. Worse, Lexi was shouting into a megaphone. "Who the hell do you think you are, taking advantage of a woman, and dumping her the next day?"

Cade's lips had disappeared into a thin white line. I could tell he was shaking. Worse, by the way his fists clenched at his side, he was about to lose it.

Lexi sauntered toward him, pointing the megaphone at his ear. "You football players think you can use and abuse any female who crosses your path."

Cade chopped his hand through the air. "That's not true."

"Do you deny—"

"Stop!" Lisa shouted, pushing between them.

Lexi batted her on the shoulder.

"You hit my roommate!" I shouted, moving into the center of the crowd, elbowing my way next to Cade.

Lisa didn't even flinch. "I have new evidence."

"New evidence, you say?" Lexi hollered into the megaphone while the crowd jeered. "Aren't you dating Jason Allen?"

"That is immaterial." Lisa wrenched the amplifier from Lexi's grasp. "Do you deny your role in setting up Cade Williams?"

"What?" Laughing like a deranged witch, the girl spread her arms. "You're insane!"

"No. I am quite in control of my faculties," Lisa said as if it were a mere matter of fact and we weren't backed against a wall. "You and your groupies—I believe you call yourself the Gyrfalcon Feathers—not only are against males who have the potential to become professional ballers, two years ago, you plotted to set up this poor man and ruin his career forever!"

"Lies!" Lexi shrieked as if she'd just been cut by a knife.

"I think not." Lisa handed me the megaphone and pulled a stack of clipped papers out from the inside of her coat. "I have in my hand proof of collusion between five women—some of whom are students or past students. But, Lexi, you were not a student here when you started seeking to ruin the life of our star tight end, were you?"

Lexi's eyes turned black and crazed. "You'd better shut your mouth."

I wrapped my hand around Cade's bicep while the campus police pulled up to the curb.

"Do you deny sending an email stating that..." Lisa smirked flipping open the document and reading, "'male college athletes think they are God's gift, and we've found our dupe. Cade Williams is going down'."

"I-I..." Lexi's eyes went wild as she looked to one of the girls holding a placard. "Men make an obscene amount of money when they go pro. It's not fair to the women athletes, or *anyone* else!"

"Right," I sniped. "And yet they make nothing when they're students while the college rakes in the dough off their sweat. Like that's fair."

"Don't egg her on," Cade whispered out of the corner of his mouth.

Lexi leered at me. "You're the last person who should talk!"

"Vivian is actually quite well versed on the facts," said Lisa while the dean stepped out of the squad car, flanked by the police. "And who better to testify to Mr. William's character than his girlfriend?"

"Jesus help me," Cade mumbled in my ear. "I don't need our sex life to be on public display."

"No effing way," I seethed, moving closer and clutching his arm tighter. There was no chance in hell I was going to testify to anything in front of these vultures.

"That's enough," said the dean, pushing through the crowd. "Disband now or face expulsion."

As Lexi started to leave, one of the officers caught her arm.

"Everyone except you." The dean pointed to the squad car. "Take her away."

Cade and I exchanged glances. "What just happened?" I asked.

"It seems, we've got quite a promising attorney in the making." The dean rocked back on her stilettos. "Lisa provided my office with proof that Cade is not only innocent, he was the victim of a plot to ruin his chances of going pro."

"Ruin my chances?" he asked his muscle flexing beneath my fingertips. "I could have done ten years hard time."

"And that would have made those women kick up their vicious heels." The dean faced him. "You are within your rights to prosecute."

He glanced at me and slipped his arm around my waist. "Hell, if I never see the inside of a courtroom again in my life it will be too soon."

"I thought as much. You're a good man, and a decent human being." The dean started off, talking over her shoulder, "Rest assured we're doing everything in our power to protect all students from being victimized—and bad things happen on both sides. But the administration is committed to uncovering the truth because the facts are the only things that matter."

"Amen to that," said Lisa.

"Thank you so much," I said, pulling her into my arms.

Cade surrounded the both of us in a big bear hug. "You're amazing, Lisa."

"Does that mean I can be your attorney after I take the bar?"

"You have to finish law school first," I said, laughing.

Cade picked us both up. "If I ever need legal help, God forbid, I know where I'm going to turn first."

Chapter Thirty-Four

Cade

After Lisa uncovered Lexi's male athlete-ruining gang and the woman was expelled, life got a lot easier. From then on, not one student said a disparaging word against me. I still can't believe she'd stooped so low. I know there are guys out there who are not respectful of women, I'm just not one of them.

Going to the combine at the end of April was the highlight of my life except I couldn't take Vi with me. I swear, once I can afford it, she's going everywhere with me. I know she wants a career, but we'll figure out how to work with both our schedules when the time comes. But now it was May and today was the first day of the NFL draft. Thank God exams were over because we were both glued to the couch.

This year the draft was in Cleveland. I could have been there, but the travel time would have cut into my last final, so I decided to be remote. I wasn't the only one. Though most everyone had been vaccinated, people still weren't traveling as much as they did pre-pandemic.

I kept looking at my phone even though it was unlikely I'd get picked in the first round. The second was possible, but I was realistic and had my hopes set on the third. But, hell, I'd take anything, including being on the practice squad of the lowest ranked team.

"Are you still breathing, dude?" Vi asked, rubbing her hand up and down my back.

I laughed, cutting her a look. "How would you feel if you were in my shoes?"

"Like I had clown feet."

"Clown feet?"

"Size fourteen, right? Your feet would look ridiculous on me."

I wrapped my arm around her neck and tugged her against me. "Always so literal, aren't you?"

"I can't help it. I'm an accountant."

"Not until next week when they hand you your diploma."

"That's just superfluous. I've passed my exams, and the CPA board. I'm in like Flynn." She pointed to the TV while the commissioner came on. "All I'm waiting for is that dude to tell us where we're going."

I released my grip and scooted to the edge of the couch while he announced the first pick—the quarterback from Mississippi who won the Heisman—no surprise there. "You know this thing goes on for three days."

"Yeah, you told me. I think we'll be certifiable by then." She stood. "You want a sandwich?"

"Sounds good." I wasn't really hungry but eating would give me something to do with my nervous energy. "Want me to help?"

"And take you away from the screen? No chance."

She was right. Jason, Devan, and I were shooting off texts between us, betting on who would be next. My money was on the linebacker from Ohio. He was a complete beast, and the only bro in our conference who had my number.

Two hours, a sandwich, and a bowl of popcorn later, the commissioner came to the stands wearing a Denver ball cap. Though it shouldn't have bothered me, my stomach did a back flip because at the combine, one of the recruiters from Denver sat with me at dinner. Not that I was special or anything. Recruiting dudes were all over the place—I mean, that's why they have the combine, so the kids coming out of college can flaunt their stuff and rub elbows with the decision makers.

"For the twenty-nineth pick in the NFL draft, Denver chooses tight end, Cade Williams, from Madison University."

"Oh. My. God!" Vi shrieked, sounding like she was in a tunnel, and surrounding me in a bear hug.

I hardly had a chance to register the news when my phone buzzed. She practically jolted off the couch. "You better get that."

I gave her a half-cocked grin and tried to swallow against the thickening of my throat while I pushed the green icon. "Hello?"

Vi sat across from me on the coffee table, biting her nails.

"Hello, Cade, this is Don Painter, coach of the Denver Stallions."

"Yes, sir."

Vi couldn't sit still, bobbing up and down like she was being prodded by electric shocks.

"We'd like you to come aboard as our first-round pick, son."

"That sounds mighty fine, sir."

"Good deal, your agent will text you with your contract and signing bonus."

"Yes, sir! Thank you, sir," I said as he clicked off the line.

I looked at Vi and opened my arms. "You want to go to Denver, babe?"

She leapt into my lap and smothered me with kisses. "Yes, yes, yes, yes!"

Chapter Thirty-Five

Vivian

The best thing about graduation ceremonies was the chance to throw my hat in the air. There were always so many speakers at these things, didn't they know, we just wanted our diplomas? But we all made the best of it. I met Cade's mother and sisters—oh my God, those two girls are identical dimes both with those stunning ice-blue eyes. Their overly-protective brother was ready to take on any football player who dared to look their way.

Mom and Grandpa were at graduation, of course. And a few days later, Cade and I packed up our measly possessions for the movers to take to Denver. At the moment, he'd taken the Harley out for a ride while I pushed the vacuum around. Honestly, everything was clean as new, but you know me, and my OCD.

I still couldn't believe it. Things had happened so fast, it was like being on a rollercoaster and hanging on for dear life. I didn't even have a chance to apply for jobs yet. If things were normal, I would have been freaking out, moving halfway across the country without a job. But the team set Cade up with an apartment and they'd already paid his ginormous signing bonus, which, we agreed, would mostly be invested. And there were plenty of jobs for accountants out west, I just needed the time to write cover letters and submit my resumé.

Cade came in, carrying a department store bag.

I unplugged the Hoover and started coiling the cord. "Where have you been?"

"Macys. Lisa met me there."

"Lisa?"

He held up the bag. "Well, I didn't know your size and stuff."

"What is it?"

"A dress."

"Serious?" I grabbed the handles and looked inside, pulling out a black dress that was sheer across the yoke and sleeves and embellished with unassuming black flowers, studded with rhinestones. "This is stunning."

From behind, he slipped his hands around my waist and kissed my neck. "You're going to look unbelievably hot in that."

I pulled the fabric. "It will fit like a glove," I said, thinking it would show every flaw.

"Lisa told me it's a bodycon design—made to highlight your curves." He ran his pinky finger in a line from my ear to my shoulder. "Problem is, I might not be able to keep myself from ripping it off you."

"And why is that a problem?"

"Because I've chartered a dinner boat for us on Lake Mendota in an hour."

I whipped around and faced him. "An hour? That's not enough time."

"Actually, you have about forty-five minutes." He tugged me toward the bathroom. "You'd better hurry."

I don't know how I managed, but I showered, curled my hair, put on makeup, and squeezed into that tiny little piece of fabric in forty-two minutes. But I dreaded looking in the mirror. Lisa knew I was self-conscious about my figure—too wide in the butt and too big on top.

At least I could wear a coat, I told myself as I cringed and turned to the full-length mirror on the bathroom door.

"Whoa."

So, this bodycon stuff worked. I mean, I think I could have passed for a movie star without a misplaced lump. Yeah, my hips and boobs were still there, but the little roll around my tummy was smoother than silk.

"You ready?" asked Cade from the other side of the door.

"I'm not sure." I turned the handle and let him have a look.

"Holy fuck." He raked his fingers through his hair, as his eyes raked down my body. "I mean. *Holy fuck.*"

I giggled, sliding my tongue to the corner of my mouth. He'd been busy too—black suit with pencil legs, crisp white shirt, and a pink tie. "You look amazing."

He waggled his eyebrows. "And I want to eat you."

"Do we have to go?"

"Yeah, but you're going to be dessert." He offered his elbow. "Come on, otherwise they'll sail without us."

But they didn't. It was a cool night that began with cocktails for two on the deck while the yacht cruised around the lake with the backdrop of a perfect sunset. As it grew cooler outside, we were ushered into a dining room with only one table set for two.

The appetizers came first, succulent crab cakes, fresher than any I'd ever tasted. "These are delicious."

"Chardonnay or Merlot for the lady?" asked the waiter, holding up a bottle.

"Chardonnay, please."

He turned to Cade. "And you, sir?"

"I'll take the same."

I waited until the man pushed through the double doors and left us alone. "This is so formal."

Scraping his teeth across his bottom lip, Cade slipped his hand into his pocket. "I wanted this to be a night neither of us would forget."

I swear he looked at me with fear in his eyes.

"Is everything okay?"

"I hope so," he said, moving out of his chair and kneeling beside me. "I've thought a lot about this, and I can't imagine ever going through life without you. You grounded me when I thought the whole world was against me. You believed in me. You pulled me out of hell and showed me that life could be fun and enjoyed and, most of all, *shared*."

My fingers trembled as I covered my mouth.

"And to top everything off, you are not only the awesomest woman on the planet, you make the best chocolate chip cookies I've ever tasted in my life." As I nervously laughed, he grinned like a stud, pulled a little box out of his pocket, and opened it. "Will you marry me? Will you *please* marry me, Vivian? I can't live—no I can't even breathe without you."

I blinked, trying to keep tears from ruining my makeup. "Yes. Oh, God, yes!"

I held out my finger and he slipped an elegant solitaire over my knuckle and kissed my hand. "I can't believe I started this year in a hole, and now I feel like I'm at the top of Mount Everest."

As he slid into his seat, I kissed him. "Maybe we're at the top of Mount Elbert—it's the highest peak in Colorado."

He greedily kissed me back, open mouthed, and raw. "You would know that."

I brushed my finger over his cheek, still shaking, hardly able to believe he was mine. "You disappointed that I'm so nerdy?"

"Never."

"I love you."

He smacked his forehead with the heel of his hand. "That's what I forgot to say." He kissed me again, this time like a man who knew what he wanted and knew how to show it. "I love you to the moon and back."

Other Books by Amy Jarecki

Epic Time Travel
Time Warriors

Guardian of Scotland time travel series:
Winner of a RONE award for Best Time Travel
Rise of a Legend
In the Kingdom's Name
The Time Traveler's Christmas

The King's Outlaws series:
Highland Warlord
Highland Raider
Highland Beast

ICE Series (romantic suspense)
Hunt for Evil
Body Shot
Mach One

Highland Force series:
Captured by the Pirate Laird
The Highland Henchman
Beauty and the Barbarian
Return of the Highland Laird - a novella

Highland Defender series:
The Fearless Highlander
The Valiant Highlander
The Highlander's Iron Will - a novella

Highland Dynasty series:
Knight in Highland Armor
A Highland Knight's Desire
A Highland Knight to Remember
Highland Knight of Rapture
Highland Knight of Dreams - a novella

Devilish Dukes series:
The Duke's Fallen Angel
The Duke's Untamed Desire
The Duke's Privateer
A Duke by Scot

The MacGalloways series
A Duke, by Scot
Her Unconventional Earl
The Captain's Heiress

Pict/Roman Romances:
Rescued by the Celtic Warrior
Deceived by the Celtic Spy

Stand Alone Titles:
The Chihuahua Affair
Virtue: A Cruise Dancer Romance
Boy Man Chief

Lords of the Highlands series:
Winner of an RT Reviewers' Choice Award
The Highland Duke
The Highland Commander
The Highland Guardian
The Highland Chieftain
The Highland Renegade
The Highland Earl
The Highland Rogue
The Highland Laird

About the Author

Known for her action-packed, passionate stories, Amy Jarecki has received reader and critical praise throughout her writing career. The author of more than 35 novels, she won the prestigious RT Reviewers' Choice award for *The Highland Duke* and the RONE award from InD'tale Magazine for Best Time Travel for her novel *Rise of a Legend*. In addition, she hit Amazon's Top 100 Bestseller List, the Apple, Barnes & Noble, and Bookscan Bestseller lists, and has earned the designation as an Amazon All Star Author. Readers also chose her Scottish historical romance, *A Highland Knight's Desire,* as the winning title through Amazon's Kindle Scout Program. Amy holds an MBA from Heriot-Watt University in Edinburgh, Scotland and now resides in Southwest Utah with her husband where she writes immersive fiction. In her free time Amy studies karate, Mandarin Chinese, and hikes the Santa Clara hills.

Find out more about Amy's books and sign up for her newsletter on https://amyjarecki.com.

CPSIA information can be obtained
at www.ICGtesting.com
Printed in the USA
LVHW042057130721
692597LV00011B/358